"IT WAS A DEVILISH DAY WHEN I MADE YOUR ACQUAINTANCE."

"Indeed, my lord?" She dimpled.

He caught her wrist and swung her expertly onto the floor. She had planned to move awkwardly in his arms, but it was impossible. Dancing with him was like dancing on air. Yielding, she let him sweep her around the ballroom.

As if he felt her soften, he drew her closer. "You are an exquisite dancer, Lady Felicia."

Deliberately she trod on his foot.

"Can't you be a good girl?"

"Not where you are concerned! Also, I am not a girl, I am a woman."

He laughed lightly. "For once I find I must agree with you. I am very much aware that you are a woman."

She caught her breath, her pulse racing . . .

Other Regency Romances from Avon Books

Avon Books are available at special quantity discounts for bulk purchases for sales promotions, premiums, fund raising or educational use. Special books, or book excerpts, can also be created to fit specific needs.

For details write or telephone the office of the Director of Special Markets, Avon Books, Dept. FP, 1350 Avenue of the Americas, New York, New York 10019, 1-800-238-0658.

Felicia

CATHLEEN CLARE

AVON BOOKS ◆ NEW YORK

FELICIA is an original publication of Avon Books. This work has never before appeared in book form. This work is a novel. Any similarity to actual persons or events is purely coincidental.

AVON BOOKS
A division of
The Hearst Corporation
1350 Avenue of the Americas
New York, New York 10019

Copyright © 1993 by Catherine Toothman
Published by arrangement with the author
Library of Congress Catalog Card Number: 92-90432
ISBN: 0-380-76816-X

First Avon Books Printing: January 1993

AVON TRADEMARK REG. U.S. PAT. OFF. AND IN OTHER COUNTRIES, MARCA REGISTRADA, HECHO EN U.S.A.

Printed in the U.S.A.

RA 10 9 8 7 6 5 4 3 2 1

For Mother and Jeff

1

London
Spring 1816

THE FLICKERING FLAMES from the fire and the warm glow of the candlelight illuminated the faces of the three young men sitting by the hearth. Outside an unusually cold March wind buffeted the fashionable London square and whistled down the chimney, sending an occasional puff of smoke into the room. But the trio didn't care. They were too well comforted by the rich supper they had eaten, the port they were drinking, and their own conviviality to concern themselves with the elements. After a spirited discourse on the Battle of Waterloo and the banishment of Napoleon, they turned their attention to subjects closer to home. In particular they discussed their friend, the Earl of Carlington, who had recently returned from the battlefields of Europe.

"The war has changed Shan," Viscount Thomas Garland pronounced. "He isn't a bit fun anymore. He only plays for small stakes, he won't race his horses, and he doesn't drink enough to make a schoolgirl cup-shot! In the past he'd never have

1

gone to dinner at his sister's house instead of being with us! Damme, if he ain't become a bore!"

Sir Everett Halloran shook his head. "I don't think it was the war at all. Didn't he get just as foxed as the rest of us the day he came home? No, it wasn't the war! It happened when he took his seat in the House. He got interested in social matters. Old soldiers and unemployment and all of that!"

"Both of you are wrong." Their host, the Earl of Grassham, refilled his glass and passed around the bottle. "It happened when his father died, and he became the earl. Lord Carlington was always stuffy and dignified. Remember how the old curmudgeon used to look down his nose at every hint of scandal? That's how Shan thinks he's supposed to be now."

"The devil he does! He's got you for an example, Marcus! You're an earl and you sure ain't stuffy! It was the war."

"I can be dignified, Tom," the young nobleman said archly.

"Of course you can. I didn't mean it that way. You can be dignified in polite society and a hell of a lot of fun outside it! So can we all, but Shan's becoming the same way in either one. He's lost his sense of the outrageous."

"So let's involve him in some sort of caper that will cause him to regain it," Sir Everett ventured. "Otherwise, we'll just have to take him as he is."

They fell silent, each considering the suggestion and remembering the way their friend had been. Shannon Carlington had been the ringleader in their most notable exploits at Cambridge. When they came to London, he had been a regular out and outer, frequenting the gambling hells, drinking to excess, and delighting in the favors of the

Covent Garden Cyprians, just like any other young lad on his own for the first time. As they gained in town bronze, he had cut a fine style, be it with the Corinthian, the *bon ton*, or the demi-rep sets. Then he went to war, ascended to the earldom, and become the haughty, cool, sophisticated gentleman he was today. They missed their old friend and wanted him back the way he used to be. He needed a reminder that life could be monstrously funny.

"I think I have it," Marcus said at last, "and this will be the finest rig anyone's ever run."

"Do tell!"

"What is the most hideous thing that can happen to a fellow?"

"Finding himself with pockets to let?" Sir Everett guessed. "And having to rusticate in the country until things get better?"

"No, no," the viscount disagreed. "That's bad, but not as awful as having to dance with your sister, and all her giggling friends, at her come-out ball. That's what *I* have to look forward to this spring!"

Sir Everett chuckled. "But that will only last a few hours, Tom. How about spending an entire Christmas holiday *en famille*, like I just did, with my sisters' brats running all over the place and yanking on my coattails? And everyone thinks it's 'sweet'! Why does a man have to withstand such torment? The awful day will come, all too soon, when you'll have to put up with your own children. Why must you be subjected to other people's urchins in the meantime?"

Marcus grinned. "Now you're coming close to the answer to my question."

"I have it!" cried Tom. "Getting caught in the parson's mousetrap!"

"Exactly!"

"Good God! You can't mean to place Shan in a compromising situation with a lady! That's no joke."

"Of course not! Just listen." The earl paused to light a cheroot, leaning back to bask in their undivided attention. "We'll place an advertisement in the paper, like people do to hire a servant. Only this one will be for a wife. We'll give Shan's name and address, and the time that the interviews will take place."

"No one will believe that!"

"No member of the *ton* will. They'll all know it's a prank, and will enjoy it to the utmost, but most of London's citizenry is not so erudite. Our ad should cause a respectable crowd of females to assemble."

"Respectable?" the viscount crowed.

Ev laughed. "Trouble is, the kind of 'ladies' I'd like to see amass can't read!"

"Never fear. The word will spread. Just see if it don't! Are we in agreement?"

The conspirators nodded.

"I'll volunteer my house as a vantage point," Tom said. "M'mother and father aren't due back from the country for two more weeks. Being straight across the square from Shan's, we'll have an unobstructed view of our results."

"Oh, no we won't! Our vision will be blocked by mobs of females!"

They laughed and passed the bottle.

"Shan will die of laughter," Marcus predicted. "If anything will shake him out of that noble manner, this will!"

Shannon Stendal, sixth Earl of Carlington, settled back to enjoy a second glass of port with his brother-in-law, the Duke of Torrence. He was attired modishly for supper at his sister's, wearing black cutaway coat, silk pantaloons, frilled shirt, and snowy cravat intricately tied *en cascade*. His golden hair was cut with precision and brushed to a rich shine. He smelled faintly of spicy Imperial water. Even so strict an arbiter of taste as Brummell could find no fault in Lord Carlington. From the top of his head to the tips of his toes, his style was conservative, understated, and perfectly elegant.

Nor was his face a detriment to his figure. Considered a prime catch on the Marriage Mart, he was frantically pursued by numerous anxious mamas who cast their eligible daughters in his path. The young ladies did not object. In addition to his title, his wealth, and his bearing, he was acknowledged to be one of the most handsome men in England.

The earl and the duke had been companionably discussing the problem of refugees from the country fleeing to London in search of employment, when Lord Torrence broke it off and smiled rather self-consciously at the younger man.

"I hesitate, Shannon, to bring up this subject. It isn't really my affair, but Eliza made me promise. Considering her delicate condition, I could scarcely refuse."

Shannon grinned. Despite his sister's recent announcement of her pregnancy, he doubted that she was as delicate as she led her doting husband to believe. Eliza had always been manipulative. Her interesting condition merely provided her with another weapon which she would wield with skill upon her victim. Not that she really needed it. Young Lady Torrence had always been able to twist the duke around her little finger.

"Eliza, and your mother, too, are extremely concerned about your finding yourself a wife."

"Here we go again," the earl sighed. "I thought they had given up."

"Not hardly," said his brother-in-law dryly. "I hear it from morning till night."

"I'm sorry, Edward. I knew that you would regret asking Mama to live with you! One woman in a house is more than enough. Two overtax the brain."

"It's not so bad, really it isn't. Eliza and her mama are good company for each other. The three of us get along quite amiably together."

The young earl nodded. Eliza and their mama were as alike as two peas in a pod. Both of them were high sticklers for decorum, and both had shamelessly henpecked their husbands. Evidently, Torrence didn't mind living under their thumbs. He must be the soul of patience.

Shannon was not. Those two ladies were enough to drive a man insane. When he was around them, he had to concentrate very hard to keep from becoming short of temper.

"Nevertheless, Edward," he said, "I am responsible for mama. If it becomes necessary, she can move in with me."

"It won't." The duke smiled suspiciously. "Aren't you changing the subject?"

Shannon laughed. "I suppose I am, but I've nothing more to add. Just tell them that I will certainly marry . . . when I find the right lady!"

"They . . . uh . . . are prepared to assist."

"Oh, no, Edward, no! I shan't fall victim to one of their schemes! I can just imagine the type of lady they would choose for me. I won't allow it." Lord Carlington tossed down the remainder of his port in a gesture reminiscent of his earlier days.

"Assure them that I attend enough social gatherings to be made aware of any eligible candidates, but I won't go to Almack's, and I won't have my mother and sister choosing my bride!"

"Shannon, they are merely trying to be helpful."

"Is that what you consider it? They are meddling as usual. I would have thought that they'd have been satisfied with my current improvement."

"Oh, they are. Definitely! But seriously, you should be thinking about setting up your nursery. You are an earl. You have a distinguished military record. You're on your way to becoming a very respected member of the House. Such a man needs a suitable wife and hostess, and a family of course. I'm proud of you, and so are Eliza and Lady Carlington. You've come a long stride from the way you used to be. You're steady, Shannon, and respectable."

"Good God! Am I that boring?"

"Not at all. When you spoke the other day in the House, of the certain fate of young farm girls who come to the city, you were listened to! I saw no member sleeping. You were intelligent and perfectly knowledgeable on your subject. The lords were impressed."

"Prior experience with some of those farm girls aided my cognizance in the matter," Shannon said wickedly.

Lord Torrence raised an eyebrow. "Perhaps it did, but those days are past."

The duke was right. Shannon's rakish days were ended. They had fled on the battlefields of the Continent, where he'd seen men who had been horribly hurt and others who had died.

He recalled with shame the day he had joined his regiment. The only thing on his mind had been to locate a source of amusement. He hadn't been interested in the condition of his troops, the state of their rations, or their strong points and weaknesses. He had been concerned only with his own entertainment, a prospect which promised very little.

In exactly two days, the regiment had been called forward to engage the enemy. He could still feel the cannon fire shaking the ground and vibrating in his breastbone. He had been so terrified that he could scarcely keep himself from galloping away in the opposite direction. And even worse, his regiment had looked to him for orders. To him, Shannon Stendal, the black sheep of the great Carlington family! Had his soldiers known what kind of man he had been? If so, why had they even given him a chance?

He remembered his father's insistence, force actually, in making him join the Cavalry. The old earl had even threatened to cut off his allowance. "Every young man should serve his country!" that termagant had ranted. "It'll be the making of you!"

And so it was. Shannon wasn't sure whether the success of his regiment was due to his own leadership, or to his men's leadership of him. That first battle proved how little he knew of military strategy, but his troops had rallied and educated their commander under fire. He'd learned from them and never forgot it. The dispatches to England became full of the wily exploits of Stendal's Regiment, and Shannon wondered why he had been satisfied, previously, with such a trivial, shallow, childish life. He was a grown man, but he had never before acted like one. Now he had the chance to make up for all those foolish pranks.

When the war was over, he hadn't forgotten his

comrades-at-arms. His major concern was not the fate of naive country girls. It was reserved for the veterans, particularly those who were disabled, and those without homes or employment. England hadn't welcomed home those heroes, many of whom now lived and died on the streets of London. The earl's staffs at Carlington House and Thistledon Hall swelled with ex-soldiers, as did that of Torrence and several others he had been able to involve. But it wasn't nearly enough, and he was putting his time and money into finding a solution. A wife for the Earl of Carlington was a matter that could wait.

But he was curious. Forewarned was forearmed. If Eliza and Mama were pushing the issue he might very well find himself caught in their net.

"I assume by all this that they have someone in mind."

"Of course." Torrence grinned, refilling their glasses.

"Who is she?"

"The Lady Penelope Hampstead, the daughter of the Marquess of Baywater. Do you remember her?"

He didn't. Certainly he knew Lord Baywater, a strong bastion of the Tory party. He must have met his daughter at some social engagements, but he couldn't place her. That was a bad sign.

"You danced with her at the Winslow affair."

Shannon shrugged. "I danced with a lot of young ladies."

"Well, perhaps Lady Penelope's face isn't particularly memorable."

"Ah! An antidote!"

"Not precisely." His brother-in-law had the grace to act uncomfortable. "She's not a Beauty, but her other attributes more than make up for a lack of countenance. Looks aren't everything, you know."

"I suppose you'd better tell me about her."

"She's of medium height, dark-haired, brown-eyed, a quiet, properly behaved lady. She's intelligent and, from being Lord Baywater's daughter, she's well informed on the political situation."

"A bluestocking!" Shannon said with disgust.

"I wouldn't say that. Believe me, there are times I've come home from the House and wished that I could have discussed the proceedings with Eliza. Not that I'm complaining of course!" Torrence smiled fondly. "Other than in matters of serious conversation, your sister and I have a very good marriage. She's just a bit empty-headed at times."

"That's certain!"

"Lady Penelope would also make you an excellent political hostess," the duke advised. "She wouldn't be gossipy. Anything could be said in her drawing room and it would not be repeated. She'd know to keep her mouth shut."

"A paragon of virtue?"

Torrence allowed himself a small laugh. "Suffice it to say that Lady Penelope would make you a very good wife, Shannon, and think of what her father could do for you! She's his only child, so he'd go all out for his son-in-law. Your career in the government would be assured!" He leaned forward eagerly. "If Lord Baywater took an interest in your social concerns, there would be something done about all this unemployment. The man has power."

"I know that, but I'm not so sure I wish to sacrifice myself on the altar of the poor. There are other ways, besides marriage, to bring about change."

The duke ignored him. "You'd probably have a cabinet position in no time at all."

Shannon narrowed his eyes. "You, too, want me to do this, don't you?"

"A man has to look out for his career. And remember, Lord Baywater is just as wealthy as he is powerful. Lady Penelope is an heiress."

"That part of it matters little to me." Shannon sighed, nodding. "Very well, Edward, I shall give it some thought. But please don't allow Eliza and Mama to take any part in this. They should know by now that I'll run backwards at the first sign of any interference."

Lord Torrence beamed with agreement. "It's a beginning, Shannon. Surely they must be pleased with that. I'll stave them off as long as I can. And now shall we join them? I fear we've tarried overlong."

The earl rose. As he followed Edward into the drawing room, Shannon thought about what his brother-in-law had said. It seemed the Duke had fallen into step with his mama and sister! All of them wished him wed, and they probably envisioned the Lady Penelope to be most perfect for the role of the next Lady Carlington, a quiet little prig, no doubt, who would mildly go about setting an example of morality and propriety. That probably was the kind of lady he needed, to suit the life he had embraced, but he couldn't help wishing that she would be pretty and a little bit of fun, too. Nevertheless, he would give Baywater's daughter a chance. Perhaps she really wasn't the ape-leader that he envisioned.

Lady Felicia Harding, daughter of the Duke of Favoringham, set aside her chocolate and pushed herself farther up onto her pillows, her sparkling

green eyes avidly surveying the advertisements in
the morning paper. "Oh, Mary, you will never
guess what is in here! What an *on-dit* it will cre-
ate!"

Her abigail, wise to the Harding family's excessive enjoyment of merriment, hid a shudder and
continued to make ready the implements of her
lady's morning toilette.

"It is an advertisement . . . for a wife! Interested
females are to apply to the Earl of Carlington at
his house this very morning. My goodness, Mary!
Do you know who he is?"

"No, my lady."

"Why he is the most odious of men! He is arrogant and conceited . . . butter wouldn't melt in his
mouth! He was reputed to have been a complete
rake in his younger days, but I cannot believe it.
He is so . . . so . . . lofty!"

"Is he an old man, my lady?"

"Hm . . ." Felicia frowned thoughtfully. "Late
twenties, perhaps, quite handsome, and wealthy,
too. But he *knows* it, Mary! He acts as though no
one is good enough for him. He is stuffy and altogether dull. I was introduced to him at the Winslow's party last month, and he acted as though he
could not wait to escape my company. I have
never been so slighted!"

The maid turned her face to hide her smile.
"Perhaps the dashing and more spirited ladies do
not catch his fancy."

"I daresay!" Felicia tossed back the covers and
slid from the big, high-poster bed. "Let us hurry to
make me ready. I fear I will be too late to be
among the first applicants."

"Lady Felicia! You cannot mean to go there!"

"Indeed I do. I wouldn't miss seeing this prank
take place for anything! I only wonder who had

the *savoir faire* to initiate it? Can't you imagine the women who will attend?"

"Yes I can, and for that reason I do not think you should go. It isn't proper! His Grace would be very displeased with you."

"Papa would find it hilarious!"

"Yes, my lady, if *he* was the one who witnessed it. He would find your own attendance improper!"

"Fustian! Papa is not such a prude!" Felicia sat down at her dressing table and began to brush her bright gold hair. "You may come along with me. Won't that lend respectability? And I won't mingle with the crowd. I shall watch only from a distance. Will that assuage your notions of propriety?"

Sighing, Mary took the brush from her mistress' hand and began to tend the shining locks, wishing that Felicia's mother had not died before she could take her offspring in hand and make a true lady of her. Lord Favoringham certainly hadn't made the least effort to curb his daughter's unbecoming high spirits. But she, as the young lady's maid, could do no more to influence her charge then she already had. Indeed she often went further than a woman in her position should go.

Pretty Lady Felicia was a hoyden. The young men enjoyed her company, but that was as far as it went. Their betrothal rings graced other fingers. It was a shame, for at heart the young lady was sweet, kind, and thoughtful of others. She was simply too headstrong and too lively for her own good.

Mary knew that only trouble would come from their presence at Carlington House. But she was just a servant, and must follow her mistress' orders. When Lady Felicia set her mind on a certain course, it was impossible to change it.

2

T HE NOISE FROM the street outside Carlington
House was muffled by the imposing brick
mansion's thick walls, but it was enough to capture the butler's notice. Never in all his years of
serving the Stendal family had Mr. Cole ever
heard such a din. The quiet, distinguished square
seemed to have burst at the seams with activity
and confusion. Curiously, he pulled back the sheer
silk curtain from one of the sidelights of the door
and peeked out. The blood drained from his face
as his quick glance became a stare of astonish-
ment. He turned slowly to face the first footman.

"It's women, Kemp."

"What?"

"Women! Females! They're all over the place!"

"What the Hell . . ."

"Mind your manners, Kemp," he said severely.
"You are no longer on the battlefield!" Lifting the
glass curtain, he drew it aside. "See for yourself."

The footman did, coming face to face with a bra-
zen redheaded woman who was peering in. "My
God!"

The butler let the curtain drop as though it were
on fire.

"They're on the stoop, sir!"

"How perceptive you are." Mr. Cole sniffed. "They are not only on the stoop, but they are on the walk and in the street."

"Per'aps it's something to do with one of His Lordship's programs."

"Well, it won't do! I won't have it! Neither will His Lordship!"

"What are you going to do?"

"I shall disperse them at once! Help me into my coat."

Kemp held the dignified black garment while Cole haughtily slipped it on. The women near the door had began to chant, and soon it was picked up by their sisters in the square.

"Nine o'clock! Nine o'clock!"

"I wonder what that means?" the footman mused.

"It means that they will wake His Lordship and he will be as angry as a stuck bear! He had a late night yesterday at Lord Torrence's home." He drew himself up to his full five feet, nine inches, took a deep breath, and wrenched open the door. "Stop this! Stop it at once!"

His toplofty command fell on deaf ears. Seeing the door open the crowd surged forward, pushing the women on the porch through the portals and into the hall. The force of the invasion knocked the butler backwards into the footman and both went sprawling onto the costly Aubusson carpet.

"Help!" screamed Cole, scrambling to his feet.

"We're being attacked!" Kemp shouted, his war injury making him rise a bit more slowly.

With the door still open, the mob continued to stream inside with great shoving, cursing, and hair-pulling. Mr. Morris, the earl's secretary, rushed into the hall, followed closely by three more of the earl's footmen. They all froze in their tracks, their mouths dropping open, when they saw the crowd of pressing women. Cole leaped to the door.

"Help me, you damned idiots!" he cried, dropping all vestiges of superiority. "Get the door closed!"

Outside, the throng's agitation had reached epic proportions. Frenzy prevailed. Senseless to each other's elbowings, kicks, and punches, the shrieking females continued to storm the door.

"Push!" shouted Mr. Cole as Kemp, Mr. Morris, and Smith, the second footman, came to his aid. "Give it all you've got, laddies!"

Together, the four barely managed to close the heavy oak door and shoot the brass bolt into place. Gasping for breath, they leaned against it and surveyed the shambles before them. The hall table had been tipped over, and its priceless Ming vase lay shattered in a puddle of water and crushed flowers. A large potted palm had been toppled, and its soil ground into the carpet. Females were breaking and using the delicate Chippendale chairs as weapons against each other, in a macabre version of medieval swordplay.

"What'll we do about them ladies?" Smith asked.

Recovering his poise, Cole favored him with a look of elegant disgust. "You will see."

Ducking blows, he made his way through the mob, gained the second step of the stairs, and squared his shoulders. "Quiet please!"

Ignoring him, the women continued their brangling.

"Quiet! We must have order! Cease this fighting at once!"

A chair leg flew past his head. Directly in front of him the brassy redhead seized the hair of her opponent and came away with a huge handful of filthy, yellow frizz. In return, the blonde bit her on the arm and kicked her shins. Mr. Cole gripped the railing and looked on with horror. Somehow the Watch must be summoned before Lord Carlington's house was reduced to kindling.

Kemp, his left eye becoming alarmingly red, joined him on the steps. "Shut up, you blasted bunch of doxies!" he shouted. "Shut up!" None too gently, he planted his foot on the redhead's bottom and sent her plummeting, knocking down women like dominoes. "Order! Now!"

Seeing a man who was not averse to tearing into them himself, the women gradually quieted.

"There now, Mr. Cole," the ex-soldier said with pride.

The butler nodded weakly and addressed the females. "Pray tell me what is going on here! What do you want?"

The hefty redhead hauled herself to her feet. "We're answerin' that ad in the newspaper!"

"Advertisement?"

"Don't you be playin' dumb with me. I know yer kind! We're answerin' that ad for a countess. Maybe you got someone else in mind, but we all get a chance! Me, I know how to please a gentleman." She preened.

Kemp snickered and received a sharp jab to the ribs.

"I am sure that there has been some mistake," Mr. Cole said helplessly. "Lord Carlington would not advertise for such! There is Mr. Morris, the earl's secretary. He would know if there is any truth to this. Mr. Morris, please come here and speak with the ladies!"

* * *

The sounds of shouting broke through into Shannon's slumber. Sitting bolt upright in the bed he looked around wildly, thinking he was on the Continent again and being attacked by Napoleon's regiments. The sight of the blue velvet hangings on his bed soothed that notion, but they didn't explain the rabble he heard.

He swung out of bed, shrugged into his robe, and crossed the room, meeting his valet hurrying from the dressing room. "What's this racket, Charles?"

Charles Freeman, who had been His Lordship's batman throughout the conflict, stared wide-eyed at him. "It's women, sir."

"Women?"

"I saw them from the window."

The earl hurried to look out. "Ye Gods!"

"Exactly, sir. What do you think they're doing?"

"I don't know, but it appears to be centered on this house. What on earth . . ."

He watched as the mob surged forward, then broke into fragments, fighting and pushing each other. The neighborhood's entire attention was focused on the small square before their houses. Aristocrats and servants alike were pressed to the windows. The staid and elderly General Winterfield, attempting to enter his carriage, was jostled down onto the pavement. Rising, he mounted a spirited defense with his cane, while a cohort of his footmen aided his return to the mansion.

Shannon shifted his gaze to the Garland House across the way, and was able to make out three forms standing in the big bow window, doubled up with laughter. He frowned. The trio was sure to be Tom Garland, Ev Halloran, and Marcus Grassham, and this scene had the unmistakable odor of their involvement.

"It's some sort of a prank, Charles."

"A prank! It's a full-scale riot! But how do you know it's a prank, sir?"

"I know." The earl's lips tightened. "The fools! Someone could be hurt."

"Here comes the Watch!"

The guardians of London burst into the square. At their appearance, footmen and ushers poured from several of the grand homes to assist them in restoring order. The general appeared again, flanked by an army of servants, and quickly cleared the street in front of his house while his wife looked on from the doorway, a parasol held at the ready position.

"Well, it won't last much longer," Shannon murmured. "Since it appears to be my fault, perhaps some of our 'old soldiers' might like to join in the fray."

"No doubt they would, sir!"

He opened his bedroom door and heard strident voices echoing up the stairwell from his own front hall. Stopping dead in his tracks, he exchanged a horrified look with his valet. "My God, they're in the house!"

"Come back inside, sir! We'll barricade the door. We'll hide under the bed."

"Nonsense," Shannon said crossly. "I'm going to stop this right now!"

"Sir! We're outnumbered and outflanked!"

"We'll see about that." He strode purposefully down the hall with Charles following nervously behind him.

He reached the gallery and looked speechlessly down on the carnage. His beautiful hall was wrecked. Trampling the ruins was a throng of the most disreputable women he had ever seen. They were fairly quiet now, but it was a surly sort of order as they listened to the reasoning of Peter Morris who, with Cole and Kemp, were blocking the stairs.

Suddenly one of the females looked up, saw him, and began to scream with excitement. "There he is!"

Lord Carlington, very inelegantly, took to his heels and ran.

Felicia Harding, hiding behind the remains of a potted plant, burst into laughter at the earl's abrupt flight. The mob had absolutely terrified him out of his wits! Alarmed at first when she and Mary had been swept into the mansion by the great mass of pushing, unwashed humanity, she was glad now that it had happened. She wouldn't for the world have missed that shocked, pinched expression on Lord Carlington's face! But now she must look toward her own safety.

The fighting had erupted again, but the earl's staff had had time to regroup itself. A large, burly maid manned the front door while a bevy of footmen and ushers propelled the women out one by one. The only other female member present was a corpulent cook armed with a rolling pin, which she spared no scruples in using. Felicia had no desire to tangle with any of them.

Her hand fell on a doorknob behind her. "Quick, Mary!" she whispered to her abigail. "In here!" As hurriedly and unobtrusively as possible, she opened the door and darted into a salon, her maid following. "We'll go out the window," she said, pausing to catch her breath.

Her white-faced abigail rushed to draw back the draperies. "Oh, my lady! It's the Watch!"

"The Watch?"

"They're arresting people!"

Felicia flew to the window. "Oh, no! We can't leave. Not yet!"

Mary began to cry. "I'll be fired!"

"No, you will not! You know Papa's appreciation of a good joke. Besides, we're not caught yet!" Wringing her hands she began to pace the floor. "We simply must wait until the square is cleared before making our escape."

"We'll be discovered by then! You know the staff will search the house. What will become of us? Your reputation . . . My lady, you must not be found in the house of a bachelor!"

"Don't be concerned with that! Would you rather enter the square and be taken to gaol? Personally, I would rather take my chances on discovery by Lord Carlington. He is so arrogant and cold that he would be sure to hush up any hint of scandal. But we won't be caught!"

"How can you be so sure?"

Felicia smiled confidently. "His staff will be so weary from their exertions that they will make only a cursory search. And we will be very well hidden! They won't see us, I promise. Come here." She caught her maid's wrist and led her to a window. "Get behind the drapery."

Mary gratefully complied. "Can you see me, my lady?"

"Not at all! And furthermore, we will be able to see when the coast is clear enough for us to escape through the window." Quickly she hid herself behind the opposite panel of burgundy satin. "Now we must be very quiet. Don't worry, Mary. We'll be back at Favoringham House in time for luncheon!"

The wait seemed interminable. Felicia's legs began to ache from her forced immobility. She hoped that poor Mary was not as miserable and decided that her abigail was probably stronger because of the nature of her work. It couldn't last much longer. The salon door had opened and closed several times and there had been footsteps, so evidently it had been assumed that the room was vacant. Now, if only the Watch would finish its task in the square!

To keep her mind from concentrating on her discomfort, Felicia reviewed the events of the morning. It was too bad that the earl's pretty hall had been damaged, but he could easily afford to restore it. The look on his face had been priceless. Never in her wildest imaginings could she have pictured the disconcertment of that arrogant, sophisticated peer. If only those haughty, toplofty young ladies, who looked down their noses at her, could have seen him fleeing madly in his state of undress! They would not be so smug about dancing with him! Felicia unsuccessfully tried to stifle a giggle.

"What is so amusing?" a cold voice demanded, as the drapery lifted to reveal her.

Felicia's stomach fell to her toes. Biting her lip, she stared into the amazingly blue eyes of the Earl of Carlington. "I . . . I . . ." Suddenly the hilarity, and not the gravity, of the situation struck her, vanquishing her fear. She burst into laughter.

He caught her wrist and jerked her roughly from her hiding place. "Who are you, and what are you doing here?"

The pain of his grip turned her humor to anger. She shook herself free and rubbed her arm. "How dare you!"

"How dare I?" he asked sarcastically. "How dare I, you little trespasser? Would you prefer that I call the Watch?" He swiveled on his heel and started for the door.

"Oh no! Wait!" Felicia hurried after him. "I would prefer to take my chances with you!"

"Oh you would, would you?" He turned to face her. "Then you had better answer my questions!"

"Yes, my lord," she replied, unable to keep a hint of laughter from her voice.

"I repeat, who are you and what are you doing in my salon?"

"We were introduced at . . ."

"I doubt that! No young lady who would be introduced to me would be caught hiding behind my draperies."

"Well, you are wrong." Irritation replaced her mirth. She was the daughter of a duke, and he was nothing but an earl. How dare he act so overbearing?

He raised an eyebrow. "If I have ever been introduced to you, I do not remember."

"Of course you do not! You didn't give me the time of day! You were too busy acting as though you were above your company!" she snapped.

A brief smile flitted across the earl's lips. "So you fancy yourself slighted? Is that why you have come here to make application for the position of Countess of Carlington? That is why you are here, isn't it?"

Felicia lifted her chin to an impressive angle. "I came to see you get your comeuppance. To be your countess would be most distasteful."

"There are many who would disagree."

"Oh, you are an odious man! A most insufferable, conceited . . ."

"I understand, Miss . . ."

"I am Lady Felicia Harding," she said with an arrogance that she hoped would match his.

"Favoringham's daughter?"

She inclined her head.

"Well, Lady Felicia, you may be my countess yet. In being here you have hopelessly compromised your reputation. Mine, too, I suppose. Now what am I going to do with you?"

"You will do nothing. When the square clears, I shall escape through the window and be on my way!"

He shook his head. "It won't serve. What if my neighbors see you?"

"Oh," said Felicia. "I hadn't thought of that. But I do have my abigail with me. Won't that lend propriety? Come out, Mary. I daresay you are weary of breathing the dust from those draperies."

"My draperies are not dusty!"

"Oh yes they are, my lord. Aren't they, Mary?" She eyed her trembling maid, who cringed against the window. "They need a good beating."

"You, young lady, are the one who needs a good beating! I shall return you to your father and advise him to do just that!"

"My father has never in my life beaten me," she said airily.

"More's the pity!"

Felicia was growing very tired of fencing with him and there seemed to be no end in sight. She had to admit that he was more than her match in wordplay. It was vexatious.

"My lord," she announced, "it appears that I must enjoy your hospitality until the square is deserted. Perhaps you would fetch me a cup of tea."

"Good God! Are you to treat me like a servant!" Lord Carlington exploded. "First you trespass into my house like a common criminal, then you insult me, and now you are ordering me about as though I were your footman!"

"It might do you some good." She flounced

down into a chair. "It would teach you a measure of humility."

"I am surprised that you are even aware of that word, my lady, for you certainly lack that trait yourself!"

"And now who is insulting whom?" she flared. "Why don't you just go away and leave me in peace!"

"Am I dismissed?" He strode to the corner and jerked the bell rope so hard that it should have come loose in his hand. "You are the captive invader, Lady Felicia, and you will submit to my rules! You may have your tea, and then I shall contrive to return you discreetly to your father. I am glad that you do not consider yourself compromised, and I hope that he will not feel the opposite, for I would not marry you if you were the last woman on this earth!"

3

HER HANDS FOLDED with practiced demureness, Felicia sat quietly in the earl's closed carriage as they drew up in front of Favoringham House. They had not uttered one word to each other as they had waited, over tea, for the square to be empty of the Watch and the crowd of onlookers. She wondered if Lord Carlington were saving up for a verbal confrontation with her father. If he expected that gentleman to chastise her as he believed that she deserved, he would experience a great disappointment. Lord Favoringham would find the whole episode vastly amusing.

She glanced at His Lordship's handsome profile. It was too bad that he was such a high stickler. If he would allow himself some fun, he would be very attractive indeed. He had the bluest eyes she'd ever seen, framed with the most incredibly long lashes. She wondered if they had ever danced with deviltry.

He stepped from the carriage and lifted her down, setting her politely, but perfunctorily, onto the pavement. "I do hope that your father is at home, Lady Felicia."

"Oh, so do I! He will be very disappointed if he misses all this."

The earl's jaw tightened. "We'll see about that."

She took his arm and entered the house, with Mary trailing fearfully behind. "Murray," she addressed the butler, "Lord Carlington wishes to speak with my father. Is he at home?"

"He is in the library, my lady."

"Thank you." She turned to the earl and smiled mischievously. "So you get your wish, my lord. I shall leave you in Murray's hands. Good day to you."

"You should be locked in your room and placed on a diet of bread and water," he said under his breath, sweeping her a magnificent bow.

Felicia laughed and started up the stairs. "I hope you will not be severely disappointed, for that will never happen!"

She had barely finished changing from her street dress to a pretty yellow gown, when she received a summons to appear in the library at once. The earl's discussion of her behavior hadn't lasted long. No doubt her father had summarily dismissed him and was now ready to laugh with her over the entire episode. But when she cheerfully entered the library, she saw with horror that Lord Carlington was still there, nursing a glass of brandy, a grin tugging at the corners of his mouth. Worse than that, the duke was regarding her with a very stern expression on his face.

"Well, missy," he said stentoriously, "I hear you have been up to mischief."

"Father, I merely . . ."

"You will apologize to Lord Carlington."

"Apologize! For what?"

"You have behaved like a hoyden at his expense and so you will beg his pardon."

"I will not!" She favored the earl with an angry

glare. "You act as though I had planned the whole thing!"

"No, Lady Felicia, I know who planned it." Lord Carlington smiled with superiority. "But your own shocking conduct has caused me immense distress."

"Oh, it has?"

"Indeed."

"Good! You need a shock! And true distress would improve you considerably!"

"Felicia!" cried Lord Favoringham. "Hold your tongue!" He turned helplessly to his guest. "You see how it is for me, Carlington?"

"Lock her in her room with nothing but bread and water," he smirked.

"I've a good notion to send her home to the country! She's no good to me here. No matter her tremendous dowry nor her pretty face, no man will ever marry her! I'll have her on my hands for the rest of my life!"

"Oh, perhaps someone, who is extremely desperate, will come along."

Watching the two men exchange smiles of mutual agreement, Felicia squared her shoulders. "I refuse to listen to any more! Perhaps I have no wish to marry. Men are the least amusing companions in the world. A dog or a cat is far better company!"

With that she whirled through the door and slammed it behind her. Fleeing to her room, she dismissed Mary and flung herself onto the bed, letting loose a flood of tears.

How could her father have humiliated her so? Why was he so treasonous as to agree with Lord Carlington's opinion of things, without even permitting her to tell her side of the story? Apologize to him indeed! At least she had avoided that. If he meant to force her into it, he would have to drag her, kicking and screaming, down the stairs. She would never apologize to that horrible man!

Oh, the odious Earl of Carlington was getting a great chuckle out of the whole matter. He thought that he had bested her, but he was wrong. She would show him! There were plenty of men who enjoyed her sense of humor. He would soon see that!

But instead of cheering her, the thought was depressing. There were men who enjoyed laughing with her, but they seemed to prefer dancing or walks in the gardens with other young ladies. She was twenty-one years old, and this was her third Season. Despite the huge dowry, no one had offered for her. What if her father was right? What if no man ever would want her for his wife?

Felicia wanted a husband. She wanted to love and be loved by a handsome, dashing gentleman, to make him happy, and to have his children. Was it too late for her? Had her excess of high spirits ruined it all? She turned her face into the pillow and sobbed.

Shannon Carlington did not go straight home after he left the Favoringham establishment. He began calling on his neighbors to offer his apologies for having innocently created the havoc in the square. It was the least he could do to make up for their inconveniences.

Mrs. Winterfield received him coolly, did not offer him refreshment, and proceeded to give him a dressing down. Apparently in her eyes, he was not a war hero, nor a respected member of the House of Lords. He was still the rakish scamp he had been in his youth. She proved this by dredging up memories of past exploits, some of which he had

been guilty of and some of which he had not. In
closing, she threatened to enlighten his mama
about his conduct.

At the next house his reception was so much the
same that the earl dreaded his third stop. It was
the home of Lord and Lady Baywater and their
daughter, Penelope, to whom his family hoped to
see him betrothed. Well, no matter what his welcome, he might at least see how the young lady
looked.

He needn't have worried. Lady Baywater was
quite pleased to entertain him. She, at least, didn't
know or didn't care that, long ago, he and his
friends had hired a troupe of opera dancers to per-
form in the center of the square, creating a rather
shocking burst of enthusiasm on the part of the
male residents. No, he didn't have to listen to that
old story again! She seated him comfortably in a
chair by the fire, ordered refreshments, and sent
for her daughter.

"I'm glad you've come by for a chat, my lord,"
the marchioness said pleasantly, "and you needn't
apologize. The disturbance did not bother us in
the least."

"I'm afraid that some of my less considerate
friends got a bit carried away, ma'am."

"That is often the case with practical jokes, but
no matter! No harm was done."

"I'm glad that you don't blame me, Lady
Baywater."

"Certainly not. How could I? Especially when
my husband thinks so highly of you."

"He does?"

"Oh yes! You are the bright and shining young
star of the government."

He smiled. "I am scarcely that, but I am honored
by Lord Baywater's approval."

"Government work is my husband's joy." She glanced at the ormolu clock on the mantelpiece. "Where is that girl?"

At that moment the door opened, and a young lady strode purposefully into the salon. She was attired in a ruffled, white muslin gown with puffed sleeves, which was entirely unsuited to her angularity. Her short dark hair was a riot of curls, unfortunately emphasizing her square jaw. Shannon couldn't help comparing her mannishness to the dainty, modish figure of the mischievous Lady Felicia. He rose.

"My daughter, Penelope. Penny, here is our neighbor, Lord Carlington."

"My lady." He bowed over her hand.

"I am pleased to make your acquaintance, my lord," she said in an expressionless voice.

"I've come to apologize for the events in the square this morning. I wish that I could have prevented it. It was a prank perpetrated by some childish friends."

"Lord Carlington is a constituent of your father's, Penelope," Lady Baywater prompted.

A tiny flicker of interest briefly lit her brown eyes.

Shannon wondered whether she would be attractive if she were dressed in a manner befitting her figure, and if her hair were styled to draw attention away from her jawline. Her eyes were not bad at all.

They sat down as the tea tray arrived. It was placed in front of Lady Penelope, who began to serve. "Sugar or cream, Lord Carlington?" she asked in a monotone.

"Just plain, thank you."

She poured the beverage without tremor of her hands, or rattling of the china, and handed it to

him. "Won't you have some cake, Lord Carlington? I've been told that it's quite delicious."

"Penelope baked that cake herself." Lady
Baywater smiled. "The baking of delicate sweets is
one of her great accomplishments."

"Then by all means, I must have some."

"Mama . . ." the girl protested somberly. "If Lord
Carlington does not wish to have cake, you must
not force him to it."

"No, I shall enjoy it," Shannon said, "especially
since I have missed my lunch. I was so anxious to
try to set things right in the neighborhood that I
forgot it."

At that remark Lady Baywater immediately
rang her little bell and sent for more substantial refreshments. "You poor dear boy, you must be quite
sharp set! Do not worry so about the neighborhood. You are doing all that is honorable. I myself
shall make certain that none think the less of you.
Penelope will help me, won't you, dear?"

"Yes, Mama."

"Thank you." He smiled at them both, and
found that Lady Penelope was the first person he
had ever seen who could receive a smile without
returning it. Was she dull-witted? Or afraid of
him? Perhaps she was simply shy.

The rest of the visit passed in a similar fashion.
He and Lady Baywater carried the conversation,
while Lady Penelope spoke only in reply to direct
questioning and in the same unaccented monotone. He wondered how his family could set her
forward as a potential match for him. Besides her
father and her pleasant mother, she had little to
recommend her. But he would give it a chance.
Perhaps with further acquaintance, Lady Penelope
would come out of her shell.

By the time he had extricated himself from the

clutches of the Baywater ladies, he had promised
to have dinner with the family and accompany
them to the theater the following evening. There
were to be no other guests, so he would have an
opportunity to learn more about the young lady.

Arriving home, he stared at his barren entrance
hall. All that remained of its earlier splendor was
the magnificent chandelier, the somewhat stained
Aubusson carpet, and a desperately frail potted
palm. He shook his head.

"A pity, sir," Cole said solemnly. "A terrible
pity."

"Yes. I dread the day that my mother sees it.
Perhaps I can replace the furnishings before that
happens. Bring me some brandy, won't you?"

"In the library, my lord?"

"No, in here." Shannon entered the salon, finding it strangely peaceful after the disturbing presence of Felicia Harding. The room should have
echoed with her repertoire of emotions.

He walked to the window and looked out upon
the square, almost surprised to find it devoid of
women. Impulsively he shook the drapery. A great
cloud of dust billowed forth. Lady Felicia was
right. The damned thing was dusty.

The events of the day caught up with him.
Thinking of that flippant little minx, the rioting
harridans, and the reactions of the neighbors,
Shannon sat down on the casement and burst into
laughter. What a tangle it had been! His trio of
friends probably felt very satisfied with themselves. It must have been their desire to give him
a great shock, and they had certainly succeeded, in
ways that they would never know.

"I am glad that someone has found amusement!
Personally, I have never been so mortified in all of

my life!" The dowager Countess of Carlington burst unannounced into the room. "Really, Shannon, stop that laughter at once! Can you not imagine my despair when I was confronted by your . . . your fall from grace? What can you have been thinking of? Creating such disorder, such notoriety! I shall never again be able to lift my head in polite society."

"I'm sorry, Mama," he said, fighting to control his amusement. "I suppose I should have warned you before the story was spread, but I have been busy apologizing to the neighbors. I'm beginning to wonder why I even thought it necessary. What happened was not my fault. It was a prank played by Grassham, Garland, and Halloran. It was all meant in fun."

"Hm! It was not amusing to me! And as for your poor sister, she was forced to take to her bed! I am filled with concern."

"Eliza will be all right as soon as she has received a sufficient amount of coddling from Torrence, and perhaps a gift of jewelry."

"You forget her delicate condition. She is most overset and, at a time such as this, the results can be disastrous." She sank weakly into a chair and lifted a vial of smelling salts to her straight, aristocratic nose. "We can only pray that Edward shall not blame you for the loss of his heir."

"Coming it a bit strong, Mama! Women have babies every day. Eliza will be fine. She's just using this as an excuse to get her husband's attention. As if she needed one! He sits in her pocket."

"And so he should! If you had a wife, you would understand."

"I doubt that." He grinned and got up to refill his glass of wine. "When I marry it will not be to a woman who takes to her bed when she feels the slightest discomfort. Nor will she wrap me round her finger!"

"Much you know of it! Now, Shannon, what are you going to do?"

"About what?"

"About the scandal, of course!"

He eyed her warily. He had already done as much as possible in his visits to the neighbors. There was nothing else to do. Everyone would know it for a joke. Unless someone had seen Lady Felicia Harding sneaking out of the house! Could that be what she was referring to?

"What is being said of it, Mama?" he asked nonchalantly.

"I do not care to repeat!"

"Come now, how may I counter scandal if I don't know what is being said?"

She pressed her lips tightly together and irritably smoothed her lilac silk dress. "Those horrible women," she mumbled. "Filling the square, coming right into this house! Fighting among themselves!"

"Is that all?"

"All! Really, Shannon, you must cut those so-called friends of yours! They have never been a good influence on you. If it had not been for them, you would never have gotten into such scrapes. I must protest your ever associating, nay, even recognizing them again. You must give them the cut direct!"

He exhaled a sigh of relief. If anyone had spread the word of Lady Felicia's adventures, Mama would have heard it by now. He was sure of the loyalty of his servants, but he hadn't been certain that they had escaped the notice of all the residents of the square.

"Well, Shannon?"

"I will consider it, ma'am."

"Good!" She nodded with satisfaction. "And the other matter?"

"What is that?"

"Your marriage of course! Torrence has informed us that you are not averse to the idea."

Lord Carlington groaned. "You'll be happy to know that I am looking over the eligibles. Tomorrow, I am to accompany Penelope Hampstead and her family to Covent Garden."

"Lady Penelope? I am pleased! A very well-behaved gel from a fine family."

"I thought you would approve, especially since you were the one who put the idea into Edward's head."

"I would welcome Lady Penelope as my daughter-in-law."

"Don't rush your fences, Mama! I've only met the young lady, and she doesn't at all seem to be my type."

"And just what is?" she snapped. "Some empty-headed little bit of fluff . . ."

"No," he interrupted coolly. "I expect my future wife to be intelligent, but I want her to be fun as well."

"Fun! A wife isn't supposed to be fun! She must take her position seriously. You can go elsewhere for fun."

He raised an eyebrow. "Really, Mama, I'd rather not."

She ignored him. "When you choose a wife, you must envision the future. You must bear in mind what she and her family will do for your career in the government, and for your standing in society. Lady Penelope would be a perfect choice."

"She isn't very pretty."

"Shannon, you exasperate me beyond all belief! Will you never be serious about this matter?"

"I am being very serious, ma'am." He smiled. "I will keep your advice in mind. I am giving Lady Penelope a chance. Won't you please be satisfied with that for awhile?"

"Very well. Just make sure that you do not do anything foolish." She rose to take her leave. "Remember, Shannon, you must always be very careful about your reputation."

"Yes, Mama."

"You have had a great many youthful escapades, which will come to light again if you allow your vigilance to slip."

"Yes, Mama." He escorted her through the house and down the walk to the curb, where her carriage waited.

"You must choose your friends with care."

"I will." He kissed her cheek. "Don't worry about me. Save your concern for Eliza!"

4

FELICIA SPENT THE rest of the day and the night in her room, mortified with self-pity. By morning, however, boredom had overcome her low spirits. She dressed in her riding habit and went downstairs, ordering that her horse be brought round as soon as she had finished her breakfast.

Unfortunately her brother, Andrew, and her traitorous father still occupied the breakfast room. She murmured a greeting, went to the sideboard, and helped herself to a heaping plate of ham, eggs, fruit, and buttered toast. Hoping that the duke would remain immersed in his morning paper, she took her place at the foot of the table.

"Ho!" Lord Favoringham chuckled from behind the *Post.* "I see that our prodigal daughter has decided to join us again."

"I assure you that it was a great disappointment to find you still here," Felicia said impertinently, stabbing her fork into the meat.

"Now, now ... Let bygones be bygones! You needed that bit of a setdown, missy."

"Well you didn't have to do it in the presence of Lord Carlington!"

Andrew smirked. "You did it in front of 'Lord Perfect'? Really, father, that was too bad of you!"

"Had to. The earl expected it! Come to think of it, young lady, you never did apologize to the man."

"I never shall! I hope I never lay eyes on him again!"

"Now, Felicia, he did rescue you from a potentially disastrous situation."

"He did nothing of the kind! If he would have left me alone I would have rescued myself. It was none of his concern."

Her brother grinned. "If I had found a pretty young lady in my house, I would have very much made it my concern!"

"Be still, Drew!" she snapped. "You know nothing of it."

"Of course I do! Father told me everything."

Felicia favored them with a malicious glare. "No doubt you both laughed over your port at my mortification! As you did, Father, with Carlington. You were perfectly outrageous and so was he. The way you both exchanged those looks of mutual satisfaction! Now let us change the topic of conversation. It is most disturbing to my stomach."

The young marquess howled. " 'Licia, I have never known you to be mortified in all my life! Nor has your appetite ever been affected by anything. Most unladylike, I might add. Instead of breakfasting, you should be suffering from the vapors!"

Trying to ignore them, she concentrated on her food. It was bad enough to have gone through the scene, without having it discussed at mealtime, especially by Andrew, who had done far worse in his short career. After all, none of it was her fault. She had merely been an innocent bystander who had been swept up by the mob. Why was everyone making so much of it?

"Carlington certainly turned the tables on you," her brother continued. "I'll wager he's never met such a female! It's a wonder . . ."

"That will be enough, Andrew," Lord Favoringham interjected, keenly watching his daughter.

"Well, if she's good enough to perpetrate a joke, she's good enough to take one on herself."

"Enough!"

"Thank you, Father," Felicia said haughtily. "This reminds me of the time you dressed as a ghost, and frightened Drew so badly that he wet his breeches. He certainly did not want to be reminded, over and over, of that."

"Good God, 'Licia, I was only ten years old!"

"Enough from both of you," the duke chuckled. "Andrew, I see that your sister is dressed for riding. Why don't you play at being a gentleman, and escort her to the park?"

"Sorry. Can't do it! I'm going to a cockfight at Willesdon. Leaving right away!" He folded his napkin and stood. "I doubt she'd want my company anyway."

"You are perfectly correct," his sister agreed. "I would rather ride with the worst criminal in London."

Their father shook his head. "When will you two ever get along?"

"When pigs fly," said Felicia succinctly, happily watching the door snap closed behind her brother.

"Daughter, daughter, you shouldn't say such unbecoming things as that! You know better."

"I'm sorry, Father. He drives me to it."

"You've been too long under the influence of a family of men. It's no wonder that you do not conduct yourself as a lady. But not to worry! I'm setting the matter to rights."

She lay down her fork. "Not a companion! Must we go through that again?"

"There will be no argument."

"Father, I know how to act like a lady, and I promise to do so. You shall never again find fault with me!"

"If there is any fault, it is with me. I fear I have treated you as I would another son. I have sadly neglected my parental duties."

"You have not! You have been a wonderful father! No one's father is as loving, nor as much fun!" she cried desperately.

"Therein lies the fault. No, my dear, it is time you became a lady in truth, as well as in title. Yesterday, after Lord Carlington left, I thought about it long and hard. I remembered a cousin of mine, a Miss Theodora Pixley, who lives alone in Hampshire. As a girl, she was very much the proper lady."

"So proper that she retains a 'Miss' before her name?" Felicia commented nastily.

The duke ignored her. "I intend to write to her immediately. Since she has no close family, I am sure she will be pleased to come to London, and provide us with her guidance."

"Oh Father, how could you ever think of such a disagreeable idea? We don't need her! We go along very well as we are!"

"Felicia, I want the very best for you. This is your third Season. You are one of the prettiest and well-dowered girls in London, and yet I see no suitors! This time, you will do as I say. And as Cousin Theodora says!"

She sighed. What a despicable kettle of fish the events of yesterday had created! She was to be forced to comply with the wishes of an antidote of an old maid, who had probably invented boredom itself, and it was all because of Lord Carlington. If he had not made such an issue of everything, she would probably have been enjoying a good laugh with her father right now. Instead, he had sentenced her to a life of certain misery.

Carlington would pay. She would never forget what he had done. Somehow, she would think of a way to get back at the odious earl.

Lord Baywater was a man who abhorred tardiness, so his party of four was seated in his box at Covent Garden well in advance of the opening curtain. With time on his hands, the great Tory leader attempted to involve Shannon in a political discussion, which was promptly squelched by his wife. "My dear, I'm sure that the young people wish to have a little chat themselves."

"But the tax . . ."

"Later," she murmured.

Shannon smiled amiably at his companion. She looked no better than she had the previous afternoon. Her pink dress, with its many ruffles and bows, would have been more becoming on someone like Lady Felicia, whose daintiness and vivacity would have matched its frills. On shapeless Lady Penelope, it was almost clownish. Why couldn't Lady Baywater, or Penelope herself, see that she should dress more simply?

He considered himself to be no expert on ladies' attire, but he certainly recognized when a female dressed nicely, and when she did not. He had half-listened to enough of his mother's and Eliza's discussions of fashion to know that one should dress to suit one's figure . . . or lack of it. Poor Lady Penelope seemed to have no shape at all. A plain, sophisticated style, with a single exquisite jewel for ornament, would have improved her appearance

immensely. If he married her, he must see that
Eliza took her shopping.

If he married her! What was he thinking of?
Now he was the one who was rushing his fences.
He must take care to proceed more slowly and not
to give her undue encouragement. It was true that
her father could do a great deal for him, but that
really mattered little when it came to spending the
rest of his life with the woman. His family had
contorted his thinking altogether too much. He
must plan on spending an evening with his
friends, soon, to dilute the influence of Torrence
and Mama.

"Do you enjoy the theater, my lord?" Penelope's
flat voice broke into his reverie.

"Indeed yes. And you?"

"I do."

"Do you come often?"

"Yes, and I enjoy the opera and ballet as well.
My father also has boxes at Drury Lane, the King's
Theatre, and Saddler's Wells. I attend one or the
other whenever possible."

"And Vauxhall Gardens, I'm sure."

She looked at him with horror. "Surely not, my
lord!"

"There are some fine entertainments there."

"Really, Lord Carlington! From what I have
heard of the 'entertainments' there, I'm sure I
would not find them to my liking. It is a scandalous place!"

"I beg your pardon, Lady Penelope. I did not
mean to insult you," he said hastily.

She drew out her fan and fluttered it nervously.
"Perhaps I have been mistaken about the place."

"I think you may have been, my lady. There are
indeed some fine musical performances on the

stage at Vauxhall. You've heard of the composer, Mr. James Hook?"

She nodded.

"He performs regularly at Vauxhall. Perhaps you would allow me to take you there?" he heard himself say.

"It might be pleasant." She smiled briefly. "I'm sure that Mama and Papa would not object to your escort. We must, however, go in company. I could never go with you alone."

"Of course not. Perhaps my sister, Eliza, and her husband, Torrence, would like to go with us."

"Very well." She folded her hands and turned her attention to the stage, where the curtain was rising.

Shannon settled back in his chair and wondered why he had ever initiated the outing. He supposed he had done it in the spirit of becoming better acquainted with Lady Penelope. He had gone this far, and he might as well see it through. Perhaps she would be different away from the supervision of her parents, but he doubted it. She was just not his style. Or was she?

He remembered Lady Felicia's nasty little comments when she accused him of being stuffy and dignified. Did he really seem so boring? Surely a career in the House didn't demand one to become staid and stolid and set in one's ways. Of course he did have to live down a previously mischievous style of life that was better forgotten, but couldn't one find some enjoyment now and then?

A movement in an opposite box caught his eye, and he witnessed the late arrival of Lord Favoringham and his baggage of a daughter. Strangely enough, she was dressed in pink like poor Lady Penelope, but there the resemblance stopped. Her gown boasted a daringly low neckline which, Shannon perceived, she fascinatingly filled to advantage, much unlike his flat-figured companion. Her golden hair was knotted loosely on top of her head, with wispy tendrils boldly escaping to frame her face bewitchingly. He wished he dared to use his quizzing glass.

Reluctantly he drew his attention back to the play and Lady Penelope. It was too bad that Lady Felicia was such a vixen. If she could behave as properly as the lady at his side, it might have been interesting to get to know her.

Felicia sat beside her father in their box at Covent Garden. To please him in his new mood, she was as demure and pleasant as was absolutely possible, but inside she was seething. An entire two days had been spoiled, and there would probably be a countless number of them to come. The ghastly Miss Theodora Pixley would certainly not turn down an invitation from the Duke of Favoringham. She would come posthaste to London and proceed to turn Felicia's life into a nightmare of postulates and namby-pamby prosings. Her father would preen, Andrew would laugh, and she would be the most miserable young lady in the world.

She could almost picture how Miss Pixley would look. She would be old, pale, and thin, a virtual wraith of a woman. She would speak in whispers and startle at the least unexpected sound. Her conversation would be of church and home, of duty and obedience. Above all, she would praise the marital state of which she knew nothing. Felicia felt nauseous just thinking about her.

The play failed to take her mind from the ordeal to come. She let her gaze wander around the theater until it came to rest on the Baywater box. Now there was a silly female if there ever was one! Penelope Hampstead was the most dull-witted, insipid, milk-and-water miss she had ever seen, but even she had a gentleman in tow. Felicia peered more closely.

She barely kept from laughing as she recognized Penelope's escort. It was Lord Carlington, and he was looking just as bored as he could be. At that moment, he was staring at the ceiling, wishing, no doubt, that it would fall in and end the farce. Penelope turned to him and spoke, resting her hand momentarily on his sleeve. His Lordship turned and answered politely, but when the girl returned her attention to the stage, he casually brushed the fabric she had touched. Felicia giggled.

"Enjoying the play, my dear?" Lord Favoring-ham squeezed her hand.

"Oh yes, Father."

"I'm pleased. You've been moping around too much of late."

"You know why," she couldn't keep from saying. "I know how to conduct myself properly, and I intend to do so in the future."

"Then you'll have nothing to fear from Cousin Theodora."

"A guest in the house can become tiring."

"I'm sure we'll manage."

She sighed. He seemed to be adamant, but she would have one more go at it in the morning. If her behavior was very, very exemplary tonight, perhaps he would change his mind. He disliked disruption in the house. She would point out how his routine might be overset.

She let her eyes drift again to Lord Carlington and Lady Milquetoast. They were far more amus-ing than the performance. She had always despised Penelope Hampstead, and her feelings had been reciprocated. That young lady had always been dull and uninspiring. In fact she was a downright ape-leader. She had constantly looked down her pug nose at Felicia, and for no reason whatsoever. The odious Carlington deserved her. Her priggish prudery should suit him perfectly.

As though Lord Carlington sensed her perusal of him, he stared in her direction. Catching her eye, he grinned.

A flush rose to her cheeks. Felicia lifted her chin and quickly looked the other way. The horrible man! Had he known all along that she was watching him? She tried to force herself to focus on the performance, but it was impossible. She glanced back.

"The cut direct?" he mouthed.

How terrible he was! He was flirting with her while in the presence of another lady! Did he think that he was so perfect that he was above all rules of decency? She frowned severely, pursing her lips, but her sense of humor soon got the better of her. She burst into laughter.

Luckily her lapse had come at a particularly humorous point in the play. Her father and the audience laughed as well. She stole another glance at Lord Carlington. He was smiling, too, but at her.

Felicia took a deep breath and willed herself to watch the actors. He was laughing at her, no doubt remembering her horrible mortification when her father had scolded her in front of him. The awful ordeal had probably satisfied him to the utmost.

She wished she could think of an excuse to leave. His presence was entirely too disconcerting. It was difficult to keep her eyes on the stage when it was so tempting to glance in his direction.

Felicia gave in to her curiosity and looked surreptitiously his way, only to find him still watching her. Lady Penelope noticed and frowned at her. Mischievously she inclined her head and smiled pleasantly at the young lady.

Lady Penelope straightened in her chair, her lips forming a pout.

Good enough for you, thought Felicia, *and you too, Carlington. I hope you marry that prune. The two of you deserve each other.*

5

DREADING THE INTERVIEW, Felicia prepared to confront her father once more across the breakfast table. After a brief greeting, he buried his face in the morning paper, as if he guessed that more unpleasantries were to come his way. Talking with the duke was not going to be easy.

At least Andrew wasn't there to make things more difficult. Experiencing another sleepless night, Felicia had heard him come in very late and stumble down the hall to his room. Her brother must have gotten himself thoroughly foxed and was now sleeping it off. It wasn't fair. Why could Andrew behave the way he did and scarcely even incite the lifting of a paternal eyebrow, while she had to endure such censure for a lesser offense?

She toyed with her breakfast and waited for the best possible opportunity to begin her discussion with her father. He would be irritable if she interrupted his news reading.

At last the duke folded the paper and laid his napkin aside. "I'd best be on my way."

"Father," she began. "I must speak with you. It won't take long."

"If it is about those bills from the dressmaker's, you may be sure that I have received them."

"Oh." She had forgotten that, and it was definitely not a good way to begin a discussion of far more value to her.

"Outrageous, Felicia. I hope that you can find yourself a rich man to marry."

"Perhaps I was a bit extravagant," she murmured.

"A bit!"

"Please, Father. I know you wish me to look nice."

"Indeed so. And you do, but so far I have seen no results."

"I don't understand." This was going badly. He had leaped in to control the conversation when she had very much wanted to guide it herself.

"I wish to see you married," he said flatly, "and as yet I have seen no man making application to me."

"I shall try harder. Now about what I wished to say . . ."

"Take young Carlington, for example. You started out on the wrong foot with him, but if you had wept and begged his forgiveness when I called you to the library, you might have caught his interest."

"I don't want his interest!"

"He's handsome and he's wealthy. Wrong political party, but I might be able to change him over. He's a liberal. A Tory with a Whig viewpoint! But what do you find so disagreeable in him?"

"He is stuffy and overbearing, arrogant, and conceited. Father, I do not wish to speak of Lord Carlington. Besides, his interest is fixed on Lady Penelope Hampstead."

Lord Favoringham began to laugh. "Don't tell me that wet goose has stolen a march on you!"

"There was no march to steal!" Felicia replied

hotly. "If I wished to attract Lord Carlington away from her, I could do so with the greatest ease! But I don't want to. She is welcome to him. They suit perfectly!"

"Spoken like a jealous hen," he chuckled.

"Father, you are being ridiculous. Let us return to the topic at hand."

"I thought this was the topic."

"We were about to discuss Cousin Theodora," she said primly.

"Oh, we were? There is really nothing to discuss about that lady. I have written to her, and that's that."

"Already?" Felicia wailed.

"The matter is concluded."

"It needn't be! You could write to her again. Please, Father! I don't need a chaperon. Nor do I need an old maid to instruct me on how to catch a man!"

"Bluntly put, my dear."

"I prefer to say what I think," she said haughtily.

"Saying and doing what you think, Felicia, has gotten you into numerous little tangles, hasn't it? No, I believe that you can benefit from the advice of another woman."

She had to change his mind, and this arguing back and forth would not do it. She had to proceed with logic. She must use her head, and not allow herself to be drawn in by petty quarreling.

"Father, you know how you hate to have the house disrupted. Having a guest will cause you to change your normal routine. You will be required to attend meals promptly, and make conversation instead of reading your paper. After dinner, you will have to take tea or coffee in the drawing room. Your library might not be sacred to you, nor will you be able to take Sunday breakfast in your dressing robe. I'm sure all of Cousin Theodora's friends will call at the house, and you will be expected to chat with them. Furthermore, you will have to control Andrew's deplorable behavior." She sat back, satisfied that she had given him food for thought.

"What about Andrew?" he demanded.

She shrugged with complacency. "For example, he came home last night— or really this morning— so disguised that he could barely flounder to his room."

"So be it! He didn't do it in the presence of his family."

"It's only a matter of time," she said smugly. "Cousin Theodora, being elderly, is probably a light sleeper. She will be sure to discover Andrew and become hysterical."

"People expect a young man to sow his oats."

"That may be, but I would certainly not allow myself to witness him in such a state. If Cousin Theodora does, and becomes overwrought, you will have to handle it yourself. I shall lock my door."

"Hm! I'll speak to your brother, and as to the rest, I will adapt myself to the woman's presence, if it will do you a modicum of good!"

"But it won't! As I have told you many times in the past, I know how to conduct myself properly!"

He shook his head.

"Give me a chance, Father!"

"No more, young lady. I know you of old. You'll simply listen to my advice, and then go out and do exactly what you please."

"I give you my word! I will even . . ." she gasped. "I will even apologize to Lord Carlington!

Just please don't saddle me with Cousin Theodora!"

"I have made up my mind, Felicia, and you'll
not change it." He stood. "I'm sorry that you are
so distressed. I believe that you're making more
out of this than you should. You may actually enjoy the company of another woman."

"Never!" She, too, rose to her feet and glared at
her father in a manner most unbecoming to a re-
spectful daughter. "This whole situation has gone
beyond the bounds of absurdity! And furthermore,
you only heard Lord Carlington's side of the story.
You never asked for mine!"

"Was there one?" he asked coldly and left the
room.

The House session concluded earlier than usual,
Shannon made his way to White's, ordered brandy,
and sat down in a deep, comfortable chair. He had
had difficulty keeping his mind on the debates today. Thoughts of his family, Lady Penelope, and,
horribly enough, Lady Felicia, kept piercing his consciousness.

He had been glad when his evening with Penelope Hampstead had ended. It was a strain to try
to carry on a lengthy conversation with her, especially after she had witnessed Lady Felicia's little
piece of impudence. The girl had been quite overset.

Shannon could sense Lady Penelope's dislike of
Favoringham's daughter. It had fairly emanated
from her. In fact it was the only emotion he had
seen her display. Unfortunately, she was no match
for the minx. Lady Felicia's vivaciousness would
always be strides ahead of her.

"Your drink, my lord."

He accepted the glass from the tray and smiled

his thanks to the waiter, sipping thoughtfully. The only saving grace of the previous evening was his conversation over port with Lord Baywater, after that interminable late supper. The man was brilliant. He could learn a lot from him. And while the marquess was extremely conservative, he had listened with patience to a few of Shannon's ideas.

"Hello, Carlington, may I join you?"

"Lord Baywater!" He rose. "Certainly, sir. I was just thinking of our talk last night."

"I hope you enjoyed yourself, m'boy."

"Indeed I did."

The marquess nodded with satisfaction. "I believe you can have quite a career for yourself in the government, Carlington, if that is what you want."

"Yes, sir."

"But I am surprised to find you here on such a mild day. What, no ride in the park?"

"I hadn't thought of it."

"You'll disappoint the ladies," Lord Baywater chuckled. "They set a lot of store by an excursion on Rotten Row. At least I know my Penelope does."

It was such a broad hint that Shannon could not ignore it. "Perhaps she will accompany me sometime."

"She'd be delighted! Go along with you now! She can be ready in a thrice. And afterwards we'll have tea."

"A good idea, sir." He set aside his unfinished drink and shook Lord Baywater's extended hand. "I'll see you later."

The interview left a bad taste in his mouth. He knew when he was being manipulated, and Lord Baywater knew he was doing the manipulating. The man was pushing hard for the match, harder

even than Shannon's own family had done. It was
unpleasant. Yet he could not, as a gentleman, have
backed away from Lord Baywater's suggestion.
He wasn't all that eager to see Lady Penelope
again so soon, but still he hadn't made up his
mind about her. However, with both his family
and Lord Baywater working the jaws of the trap,
he must proceed very cautiously.

Feeling that Lady Penelope would not appreciate his curricle, he had the landau set to and half-
heartedly directed his coachman to Baywater
House. As the marquess had predicted, the young
lady was delighted. She quickly readied herself
and soon they were on their way to Hyde Park.

"It's a nice day," Shannon said in an attempt at
conversation.

"Oh yes," she replied in the monotone he was
becoming accustomed to.

"Your father said you enjoyed driving in the
park."

"Yes."

"Do you also ride?" A riding habit would be
more suited to Lady Penelope's style. Its military
cut would eliminate all those awful fringes and
furbelows.

"No, I don't care for that."

"I see."

"I'm afraid of horses," Lady Penelope ventured
timidly.

"That's too bad. Perhaps you had a fall that en-
couraged your fear?"

"No. I have always been afraid of animals ...
dogs, cats, horses, all of them."

"It must make you uncomfortable in the country."

"I seldom go to the country, and when I do, I

take care never to go outdoors in places where animals might be wandering loose."

Shannon thought of his own estate with its plethora of animals, where his two pointers roamed both inside and out. Lady Penelope would never countenance a dog in the house. She would probably even toss out ancient Old Sarum, the cat, whose sole purpose in life was to rid the mansion of field mice.

"Do you like animals, my lord?"

"I have some very good animal friends, Lady Penelope. Animals are often more pleasant than people, you know. No matter what mood you're in, or what horrible thing you've done, they are always glad to see you."

"I wouldn't know." She shuddered. "Perhaps one could become accustomed."

"Perhaps." Their carriage joined the others wending their way through the park. "There are quite a few people here," he observed, "and the Season has scarcely started."

"Yes."

Shannon glanced ahead and his heart rapidly sank to his toes. The Lady Felicia and another young woman were mounted on horseback and traveling in the opposite direction of the carriage flow. They would be sure to pass by.

Favoringham's daughter was looking well today. Her scarlet velvet riding habit with its black and gold epaulets, and her pert hat with its flowing black plume, made her a standout in any crowd. Even the color of her mincing horse seemed to compliment her appearance. His golden coat seemed to exactly match his mistress' blonde hair. But, as Shannon knew from experience, pretty looks in Lady Felicia did not necessarily mean pretty behavior.

Dear Lord, what would the vixen say or do? After the events of the past week, something perfectly awful might happen. She obviously cared little for Lady Penelope, and she probably hated him, despite her little flirtation of the evening before.

There was nothing he could do about it. He couldn't have John Coachman back the landau around and go in the other direction. It would be too obvious to all witnesses, and would seem perfectly ridiculous to Lady Penelope. He would simply have to hope for the best and, with Lady Felicia involved, that was dangerous indeed!

Felicia could have laughed when she looked ahead and briefly met the worried eyes of Lord Carlington. She could almost read his mind. He was fearful of her causing a scene before his precious Lady Penelope. Well, he needn't be concerned. She intended to cut them both.

She stroked her horse's shoulder. "Barbara," she murmured to her friend. "I see Penelope Hampstead up ahead, and I positively despise her. I intend to give her the cut direct."

"Felicia, you can't do that! I don't like her either, but to do that would be so very rude." She glanced in the same direction. "Oh, how awful! She is escorted by Lord Carlington! How can she have captured his attention?"

"Perhaps it is because he is just as odious as she."

"I don't think he is," her friend said dreamily. "I think he's the most handsome man I've ever seen."

Felicia made a mew of disgust.

"Don't you agree? Speak the truth!" Barbara teased.

"He is well enough, but I have seen better. And I certainly have seen more charming men! Lord Carlington is arrogant and stuffy, and so is Penelope. I am going to cut them."

"Well I'm not. If my mother heard that I had done such a thing she would be mortified! Besides, he might take an interest in me. Am I not prettier than that awful Penelope?" She urged her mare forward.

Felicia followed more slowly, holding her horse so tightly in check that he tossed his head and pushed at the bit. Since it was obvious that she accompanied Barbara, she would have to stop, but she would greet them with only a small measure of civility. She certainly would not carry on conversation.

What was the matter with Lord Carlington anyway? He surely couldn't think Penelope Hampstead attractive! Yet he had escorted her to the theater last night, and here he was with her today. What attribute did the girl possess?

Lady Penelope had been on the Marriage Mart for at least two years before Felicia made her debut. She hadn't been taken then, nor should she now. She was whey-faced, dull, and boring. Gentlemen only danced with her for politeness' sake. Lord Carlington was an utter fool to have anything to do with her.

She rode up beside the landau and reined in abruptly, irritated by Barbara's gushing chatter. Lifting her nose a trifle, she looked off into the distance.

"Good afternoon, Lady Felicia," the earl said smoothly, a hint of amusement in his deep voice.

"Penelope. My lord." Hands tightening, she refused to spare them a gaze. Her horse jibbed and skittered sideways.

"If you would loosen the reins, he might stand quietly," Lord Carlington remarked.

"When I need your advice, my lord, I shall ask for it." She couldn't keep from looking at him. "I realize, however, that you are in the habit of dishing out many unwanted recommendations."

Penelope gasped.

Felicia raised an eyebrow to her. "Don't be shocked. You should know that Lord Carlington and I are old sparring partners."

Lord Baywater's daughter pursed her lips and lowered her eyes to her hands.

"Felicia!" Barbara scolded lightly. "You are too bad!"

"Indeed I am much more so, am I not, m'lord?" With a triumphant smile, she moved on.

Her friend very quickly caught up with her. "You certainly overset poor Penelope," she giggled.

"That requires little effort!" Felicia laughed.

"No, but let us not talk of her. I want to know about you and Lord Carlington!"

"There is nothing to know."

"Come now. You were jealous of Penelope Hampstead. When you saw them together, you didn't like it above half!"

"That is perfectly ridiculous." Felicia urged her horse into a trot.

"Wait!"

She slowed to a walk. "Barbara, what you are insinuating is ludicrous. There is nothing between Lord Carlington and me. Please don't spare it another thought."

"I think he admires you."

"Fustian!"

"And Penelope definitely considers you a rival. But she doesn't know what to do about it!"

"This is nonsense." Felicia felt a warm flush suffuse her cheeks. "Lord Carlington considers me to be just as odious as I consider him. And there's an end to it!"

Barbara laughed softly. "Somehow, I doubt that," she mused. "I doubt it very much."

6

WITHIN A WEEK, Felicia, sitting in the window
seat of the second-story salon, saw a hack-
ney carriage draw up in front of Favoringham
House and a primly bonneted, gray-clad female
emerge. Heart sinking, she knew who this must
be. Cousin Theodora hadn't even written a reply.
She was so anxious to aid Lord Favoringham in
putting a period to his daughter's high spirits that
she had come as quickly as she could. Felicia
sighed, set aside the novel she had been reading,
and prepared to welcome the paragon of female
delicacy and virtue.

This was all Carlington's fault. After the light
flirtation at Covent Garden and her friend Barbara's remarks, she had been inclined to look more
favorably on the earl, but that had all changed, as
of now. He would pay for causing her to be saddled with this milquetoast spinster!

She curtsied as Murray showed the old maid in.
"How do you do, Cousin Theodora? I am Felicia."

Faded blue eyes surveyed her. From her mousy
gray hair to her dreary, gray, old-fashioned traveling ensemble the woman was much as Felicia had
expected her to be. Even her deeply wrinkled face
seemed gray, surrounded as it was by so much

61

drabness. All in all, she reminded Felicia of a most unpleasant, rainy day.

Cousin Theodora murmured a weak greeting and sank into the nearest chair.

"Murray, please bring refreshment and inform my father of our cousin's arrival." Felicia sat down politely beside her and smiled prettily. "I'm sure you must be weary from your trip, ma'am."

"It was most tiresome." She brushed a languid hand across her forehead and leaned her head against the upholstery. "But any sacrifice is not too great to cause me to turn my back on my cousins' need.

"Poor child! It is a sad thing to grow up without a mother to guide one's footsteps, but have no concern. You will learn to please your papa and furthermore, I am certain that you will find the proper gentleman to be your husband. I'm sure you miss your mother, but perhaps I can be an adequate substitute."

"I don't even remember my mother," Felicia said flatly.

"Oh my, what a shocking thing to say!" She rallied from her lethargy. "Your mouth should be washed out with soap, young lady! Such an appalling lack of respect. No wonder you chase the men away."

"My mother died when I was born. How could I . . ."

"Cousin Theodora!" the duke boomed from the door, advancing with open arms. "I didn't expect you this soon!"

He would have hugged her, but she forestalled him with an outstretched hand. Pausing, he kissed the bony limb.

"Perceiving our great need, Cousin Theodora came as quickly as she could," Felicia said dryly.

"It was very kind of you, ma'am." Lord Favoringham regarded them both with a hopeful smile. "What do you think of my little Felicia, cousin? Isn't she a winsome gel?"

"Forgive my cliche, Your Grace, but pretty is as pretty does." She removed a lorgnette from the reticule and trained it on Felicia. "Beauty is vastly overrated. A proper gentleman looks for modesty and obedience in his future wife. So far, I find this young lady sadly lacking."

Felicia's eyes narrowed. Apparently Cousin Theodora was not as puling as she appeared.

"What?" The duke stared wonderingly at his daughter.

"For example," Cousin Theodora began in a voice surprisingly firm, "her gown is cut much too low for decency. No husband wishes his lady to be so exposed . . . even to himself!"

"This is the latest style!" Felicia protested, glancing down at the soft, rounded tops of her breasts. "One often sees bodices cut even lower!"

"It will not do."

Lord Favoringham frowned slightly. "Spare no expense in dressing her properly."

"I'll look like a schoolgirl!" his daughter cried.

Cousin Theodora shook her head. "And her hair must be attended. A nice modest knot at the nape of her neck and none of those saucy curls around her face! She looks like a wanton."

"No!"

"Daughter, you will obey our cousin's advice. We have asked for her guidance and it will be followed."

"People will think I'm a governess!"

"They will think that you are a proper young lady," said Cousin Theodora, with all the fervor of a missionary.

"Father, she doesn't know what she is talking about. She will make me a laughingstock!" Felicia flung herself up from her chair and began to pace the room. "I would rather bury myself in the country than to participate in this farce!"

"Felicia . . ."

"Why do you think she is such an authority? I see no ring upon her finger! She is nothing but an old maid!"

"Felicia!" the duke exclaimed, his face growing red. "You will go to your room at once!"

"I will not! I will not go meekly away and leave her to fill your head with nonsense! I am not a child! I am twenty-one years old, and I deserve to have a say in my future!"

"You are certainly acting like a child," Cousin Theodora observed. "Goodness me! I don't think I have ever seen such an exhibition from one who was bred to be a proper young lady!"

"Proper, proper!" she flashed. "Must everything be 'proper'? Proper gentlemen! Proper ladies! I swear I am sick of the word already."

"Proper young ladies do not swear."

Lord Favoringham spread his hands helplessly. "You see my dilemma?"

"Dilemma!" Felicia cried. "You had no complaints of me until that odious Carlington put a bee in your ear. You were delighted with me up till then!"

"Oh, catch hold of yourself!" Cousin Theodora snapped. "Those who wish to be treated as adults must act appropriately. Cease your prattle or I shall call a footman and have you removed!"

Felicia looked with shock at her father.

The duke shrugged. "Heed your cousin."

"Father!"

How could he side with this dried-up old spinster? Surely he knew that what she was suggesting was wrong! He couldn't be so unknowledgeable of ladies' fashions.

She took a deep breath and plopped down onto a sofa, glancing from one to the other with glaring green eyes. Lord Favoringham sagged unhappily in his chair, but Cousin Theodora sat straight up in hers, a smug smile on her lips as though she had won an important battle. There was no sign of her earlier weariness.

Felicia suddenly realized that she was facing a formidable opponent. With the duke's backing, Cousin Theodora could make her life even more miserable than she had visualized. She must change her tactics. Her childish temper tantrum would have defeated her father, but it had scarcely fazed the old lady. She must use other means to get round her. The drab spinster was stronger than she seemed.

A footman entered with the tea tray and, without hesitation, set it before Lady Felicia. Well, at least in the eyes of the servants, she was still the mistress of the house. She wondered what he would have thought if he had been ordered to carry her, kicking and screaming, to her room. She must keep the servants on her side. They could be powerful allies if worse came to worse.

"Thank you, Thomas." She offered him a brilliant smile as he withdrew. "Tea, Cousin Theodora?"

"Yes, my dear." She extended a talon-like hand. "Now isn't this pleasant? A family should always gather together for tea. Isn't your son in London also, Your Grace?"

"Andrew?" Lord Favoringham accepted a cup from his daughter. "Yes he is, but we see little of him!" He laughed as if relieved to see the conversation turning to polite inanities.

"You will find him a sad wastrel," Felicia said with inspiration. If she could direct some of Cousin Theodora's attention to her brother, she might receive a small measure of relief. At least it would be amusing. "He, too, misses the benefits of a mother's guidance. He gambles, drinks to excess, and . . . well . . . he has some activities which cannot be politely discussed. Do you not think that a young man can also benefit by the gentling of a 'proper' lady?"

"Indeed I do! Really, Lord Favoringham, you should have called upon me much earlier. A single man cannot hope to rear his children properly."

The duke looked sharply at his daughter and received a sweet smile. "Andrew is all right," he mumbled.

"Oh, Father, you know that at this moment he is probably laying his money on a cockfight or boxing match. Or worse . . ."

"I shall have a talk with him," Cousin Theodora stated. "Since I am to become a member of this household, it is only fair that he should have his share of my attention."

"He will appreciate that," Felicia said with glee.

The gray lady raised an eyebrow. "But do not think it will allow you to escape my notice, young lady. It is because of you that I am here. And when you wed a proper gentleman, you will see that I know what I am doing!" She looked at Felicia thoughtfully. "I believe that you already realize that your ridiculous tantrums will not serve. You are intelligent. It shouldn't take you long to understand that I am right, as your father has already done. Am I not correct, my lord?"

"Oh indeed, indeed." He avoided his daughter's eyes.

"Well then! All is settled! Tomorrow, Felicia, we shall shop. You will have a new wardrobe! Now won't that be fun?"

The duke groaned.

"It will not be terribly expensive, Cousin," Theodora assured him. "A few simple designs will be sufficient. Do not be concerned."

Felicia set her jaw. She could imagine Cousin Theodora's fashion ideas. She would not wear the new things. She might be forced to abandon, temporarily, her sense of fun, but she would not make a fool of herself in front of the *ton*. Unless she missed her guess, there was going to be a grand and continuing quarrel in store for the residents of Favoringham House.

In all too short a time, Felicia found herself staring unhappily at her "proper" new gowns. The pale pinks, greens, and yellows were colors she could wear, but the white muslins so beloved by Cousin Theodora did not suit her at all. With her fair hair they made her look disgustingly washed-out. Nor did the bodices compliment her well-developed figure. Rising nearly to her neck, they were almost medieval in style. How the *ton* would laugh!

"What am I going to do, Mary?" she asked sadly, as she watched her abigail remove the dresses from their tissue paper and hang them away in her dressing room. "How can I show myself in those?"

"Perhaps you'll start a new style, my lady."

"You know I will not! And my hair . . ." She gazed wistfully into the mirror at her tightly knotted tresses. "I look a fright, don't I?"

"My lady . . ."

"Don't I?" Felicia prodded.

Mary sighed. "I have seen you in better looks."

"Well, I won't wear them, and that is that! And I won't wear these." She held up a pair of uninspired slippers of rather thickish leather. "They look like something a Quaker might own! I've seen pictures of ladies of Cousin Theodora's generation, and their clothes were not like this. The woman is mad!"

Her abigail bent her head.

"How can I ever again hold up my head in Society if I wear clothes like these?"

"Perhaps, my lady, if . . ."

"Yes, Mary, go on!"

"Perhaps when His Grace sees you in these dresses, he will relent."

"I feel like throwing them out the window!" She irritably removed the pins from her hair.

"Yes, my lady, but . . ."

"Well?"

Mary seemed to shrink. "A show of temper might only provoke him."

Felicia considered. "Perhaps you are right. I'll try it. But if it does not work, there will be further confrontation. I will not dress myself up as an antidote! I would only be an object of humor." She yanked a hairbrush through her shining locks. "I shall be so mortified."

"People are too polite to laugh at you, my lady."

"I know one who is not." A vision of amused blue eyes floated through her mind. "Lord Carlington would find me vastly entertaining, dressed in this fashion."

Mary took the brush from her hand and began to stroke the curls more gently.

"He would laugh, and laugh, and laugh."

"Surely, my lady, the earl is too much the gentleman to laugh at your predicament. He would know that there is something wrong."

"And he would delight in it! This is all his doing. If it were not for him, I would be enjoying my life as usual, instead of looking like an apeleader, and listening to the moral prosings of a silly old maid all day long! Mark my words, I intend to tell him so! I shall have my revenge!"

"Maybe it won't come to that," Mary said meekly.

"Oh, yes it will! Even if I convince Father that this attire is impossible, I am still saddled with Cousin Theodora. No, he shall get his comeuppance! Now help me into the ugliest gown in my dazzling new wardrobe. I don't wish to be late to supper and incur everyone's wrath."

Andrew snickered as Felicia entered the drawing room. She favored him with a look of disgust, which enveloped her father and Cousin Theodora as well. Never in her life had she been in such poor looks. Her guinea-gold hair was pulled into such a severe knot, it threatened to give her a headache. In her ears were minute pearl earrings, suitable only for the youngest of debutantes. Her face was extremely pale, and void of cosmetics, giving her a wraith-like appearance. Her white dress completed the ghostly vision.

She curled her lip. "Well, here I am. Ready for Society! I am sure to be an Incomparable!" Whirling in a circle, she smiled dangerously. "I shall have men fainting from desperation at my feet."

"That," said Cousin Theodora, "is a most unbecoming thing to say."

"But true." Her brother laughed. "I'm desperate!" he shouted, clutching at his heart. "Take me away from this paragon of virtue!" Gurgling, he cast himself to the floor.

Lord Favoringham laughed loudly, and even Felicia giggled.

"Get up from there, Drew," Felicia ordered. "You of all people must not faint whenever you are in my presence, for you shall probably be my only dancing partner."

He got to his feet, negligently dusting his coat. "Don't count on it, sweet sister. If you are to dress like that, I shall make myself scarce at any ball you choose to attend."

"Hm!" She raised her nose. "Do as you please. I don't wish to dance with you anyway. You always step on my toes. Not that it would pain me, for look at what I am wearing!" She lifted her skirts to reveal her sturdy slippers.

"Good God! Whose shins do you intend to kick? He'll have to hobble on a cane after you get through with him."

"Thank you, Andrew. You've just given me an excellent idea."

"Let us stop this nonsense," Cousin Theodora announced. "It is time for dinner."

"Indeed it is! 'Licia, go back to your room and change. The joke has gone on long enough."

"Joke?" she asked sarcastically. "I wish it were."

"You're not going to continue to dress like that!"

"By absenting yourself from this house, dear brother, you have missed a great many of the changes here. This, indeed, is my new attire."

"Father!" Andrew protested. "Cousin Theodora, really! Felicia can't wear that! She looks like a governess!"

The duke shook his head, and all eyes turned to their gray-clad cousin.

"It is the proper dress for a modest young lady."

She stood. "You will see the impression she makes."

"You are really serious about this?" Andrew asked, astounded, looking from one to the other.

"Your sister presents a very becoming appearance."

"Father?"

"Andrew," Lord Favoringham said wearily. "I have been over and over this matter, and I do not intend to continue to do so. Cousin Theodora has assumed the responsibility of improving Felicia's manner, and I am content to allow her to see what she can do."

Shaking his head, the young marquess pressed a surprising kiss to his sister's forehead. "I'm sorry I laughed, Felicia. I'm sorry . . . about everything!"

She blinked back sudden tears. Andrew had never been so contrite. Perhaps he did possess a modicum of brotherly love. "It's all right."

"No, it isn't! It's ludicrous!" Without another glance, he started out the door. "I believe I shall dine at my club."

"Well, isn't someone going to stop him?" Cousin Theodora wailed. "At dinner, a family should be together!"

"Let him go," the duke frowned. "Come. Let us get on with this." He presented his arm to his cousin and led her to the dining room, leaving Felicia to drift along behind, her hopes plummeting.

7

THE NIGHT AIR was slightly chilly, but the ladies' cloaks and the gentlemen's coats kept them warm, as Lord and Lady Torrence, Lady Penelope Hampstead, and Lord Carlington strolled through the entrance to Vauxhall Gardens and up the Grand Walk. The elms on either side twinkled with lanterns, and soft voices laughed and talked, creating a subtle romantic atmosphere. Above loomed the tiny sliver of a new moon.

Shannon glanced down at the lady on his arm and smiled encouragingly. Lady Penelope had been hesitant up until the last minute about coming with him. In the end it had been her mother who had insisted, overcoming her daughter's fears by maintaining that she would have quite an enjoyable time. After all, wasn't her escort a perfect gentleman? And weren't Lord and Lady Torrence above all impropriety? Lady Penelope had quickly agreed, but he could tell from her tension, as she had sat beside him in his brother-in-law's town carriage, that she was not entirely reassured. Poor Penelope! Now that they had been together several times, he had hoped that, away from her parents, she might loosen her stiffness a little.

Penelope's ill opinion of Vauxhall Gardens was

incorrect. It was true that the pleasure spot attracted all manner of people, from the very fashionable to the lowest citizen who could manage the few shillings admission. And there were the Dark Walks and grottoes, where patrons might engage in rather illicit behavior. But, for a circumspect young lady accompanied by a proper gentleman, there was little to fear.

Indeed there were many delights. The Vauxhall food was good, the musical performances were better, and the fetes on special occasions were outstanding. Lord Baywater's daughter must be overreacting to the bits of scandal she had overheard. Shannon had always treated her with absolute decorum. Surely she couldn't be afraid of him.

Torrence who, with Shannon's sister, was preceding them, turned. "Shall we locate a supper box, or walk a bit more?"

"I had thought to show Lady Penelope the South Walk."

"Oh yes, do," Eliza seconded, "but forgive us. These days I am careful not to become overtired. We shall secure a box and see you later."

"I would rather come with you," Penelope said flatly.

Shannon's sister frowned. "The South Walk is so fascinating! There is a lovely vision of the ruins of Palmyra, and a little Gothic Temple . . ."

"I fear it would be improper, madam. I must stay with you."

Eliza quickly hid her dismay. "Very well, but it isn't necessary at all."

Shannon grinned at the ruination of his sister's attempt to leave them alone together, but he was vaguely disappointed as well. Evidently Penelope had the idea to ride in Eliza's pocket. At this rate he would never see if there was another side to her demure, uninspiring behavior.

"Perhaps another time," he murmured.

Lady Penelope flashed him a very brief smile of relief.

They found a box and placed their order for chicken, pastries, and the wafer-thin slices of ham for which Vauxhall was famous.

"During our courtship, Torrence and I loved to come to Vauxhall," Eliza said to Penelope. "Balls and rout-parties can be such stuffy affairs."

Shannon raised an eyebrow to his brother-in-law, who merely looked bemused.

"We also enjoyed picnics at Richmond," she continued, "where it was possible to obtain privacy."

Penelope's eyes widened.

"One can scarcely get to know each other within the confines of the drawing room," Eliza advised.

"You are shocking Lady Penelope, my love," the duke interceded. "You'll have her thinking us improper."

"Oh, no! We were not that at all! It was only that . . ."

"Here is our food," Shannon said. "You must be sure to try the ham, Lady Penelope. It is rather special."

Lady Penelope merely picked nervously at her supper. She managed little more than a slice of ham and a bite of pastry, before laying down her fork. "It was very good," she said politely, "but I am not hungry."

"Exercise would improve your appetite," Eliza remarked.

The evening passed interminably with the Torrences and Shannon carrying most of the conversation, and Lady Penelope adding very little in her dull monotone. The earl was glad when he deposited the young lady safely at her door and climbed back into the coach. If anything of value had come from this experience, it was that he had made up his mind to cool his interest in Baywater's daughter. He had seen altogether too much of her in a short period of time. If it continued, it would cause uncomfortable expectations. He was not prepared for that, especially after tonight.

Apparently, no man would become truly acquainted with Penelope Hampstead until he slipped a ring on her finger, and then it would be too late for second thoughts. Lord Baywater's patronage was one thing; marriage was quite another matter. At this point in time, Shannon didn't think he could spend the rest of his life listening to that dull monotone. The girl was a thundering bore, and he doubted that any amount of intimacy would change it. He longed to stick her with a pin to see if she even reacted to that. A curse, a show of waspish behavior, or even a slap in the face would be far preferable to her damnable apathy.

He hoped Eliza was pleased with the paragon of virtue she had helped choose for him. His sister, away from Mama, could be quite lively. Tonight she had yawned three times.

"The evening is still young, Shannon," Torrence said. "Why don't you stop by the house and have a glass of port with me?"

"Yes, do!" Eliza prompted. "I'm sure that Mama will still be up and anxious to see you."

"I shall. I have something to say to all of you."

"What is it?"

"If Mama is still about, I'll wait till then."

"I hope it is good news."

"For me it is."

His sister looked at him fearfully. "Oh dear, I don't believe this is something Mama wishes to hear."

"Probably not," he said dryly.

Lady Carlington nearly met them at the drawing room door, her excitement palpable. "My dears! You are home early!"

"Yes, Mama! We have had the most wonderful time!" Eliza chirped, edging away. "However, I find myself fatigued. I think I shall retire."

"Eliza . . ." Shannon adeptly caught her hand and escorted her and their mother to a seat on the sofa. He accepted a glass of wine from Lord Torrence and looked at the expectant faces.

"Is this to be a formal announcement?" Lady Carlington asked lightly. "Dear Shannon, is your bride to be Penelope Hampstead?"

"I don't think so, Mama." He held up his hand to forestall her interruption. "I don't believe we should suit."

"Wouldn't suit! Why, she's perfect for you! She is an heiress of excellent birth. Her manners are perfect and . . ."

"She's an antidote."

"Shannon! How can you say such an unkind thing!"

"Have you seen her?" he demanded.

"Of course I have! She might not be a Beauty, but her other attributes far make up for a lack of countenance. As to that, I do believe that Eliza could advise her on her appearance. Lady Baywater has no taste! With Eliza's hairdresser and modiste . . ."

"She is dull and boring."

"She is merely shy!"

"No, Mama, she is dead and doesn't realize it yet." He gratefully accepted a glass of wine from

Torrence. "If I am to marry, might not I find a wife who entertains me?"

"I have never heard anything so outrageous!" Lady Carlington pursed her lips with disgust. "You make it sound as though you are going to a theater!"

"It is easy for you to criticize. If you spent more than a half hour in her presence, you would go to sleep."

"I could not commit such a social solecism! Put that aside. Think of what her father can do for you."

"If that's what it takes to further my career, I'll retire to the country and forget all about it," he said firmly.

"Perhaps you haven't given her enough of a chance," Eliza ventured. "Many young ladies are extremely shy. You are so devilish handsome, Shannon, and at one time you did have that awful reputation. She is probably fearful of you. Give her time to discover your sweetness and kindness."

He rolled his eyes heavenward. "I am being manipulated by all of you and by Lord Baywater as well. If I continue to allow it, expectations will arise. I see a trap, and I don't like it!"

"Shannon's right," the Duke of Torrence said quietly.

"But . . ." both ladies began at once.

"The girl's an ape-leader," he declared over the top of their protests. "She'll never change."

"Edward!" his wife cried.

"This was the most boring evening I ever spent and you, love, must agree that you feel the same. You were looking forward to this outing, and you ended up having a most miserable time."

"Perhaps Shannon did not attempt to draw her

out," Lady Carlington accused, casting a look of displeasure toward her son.

"Shannon did everything he could, ma'am. So did we all."

"I still believe that she is merely shy!" Eliza snapped. "He has not given her a sufficient chance!"

The duke shrugged. "You have your opinion; I have mine. Mark my words, if you succeed in what you are trying to do, you will certainly drive him into the arms of a succession of mistresses. No real man could live with that cold fish."

Eliza gasped.

"Thank you, Edward," his brother-in-law said mildly. "I'm glad someone sees my side of it."

Lady Carlington stood. "I am not pleased with any of this. Come, Eliza, we shall retire." Without farewell, she led her daughter from the room.

Shannon sighed. "I'm sorry you've been placed in the middle of this, Edward. The ladies are angry."

"It was something that needed to be said. Much as I hate to admit it, you wouldn't suit." He shrugged. "Anyway I can bring Eliza 'round in five minutes."

"Sure of yourself?"

"Undoubtedly!" He refilled their glasses. "Just let Lady Penelope down easily, Shannon. I have no desire to have a quarrel with Lord Baywater."

"Don't worry. It hasn't gone so far that it can't be easily managed. I doubt that she will even notice, or care."

"I wouldn't be too sure about that. She may have formed expectations. Be careful."

"I shall," he promised, feeling a surge of relief. "Everything will be all right."

* * *

Felicia stood, hands on her hips, her green eyes glaring. "You have read *La Belle Assemblee*, Cousin Theodora! Surely you can no longer be fooled on the current fashion! These dresses are impossible!"

"Fashion journals exhibit the most outlandish of style. No one wears such clothes. No one *I* care to know, at least! There is a small segment of the population who may indulge in such shocking attire, but you may be assured that the Favoringham family is not a part of it!"

"The demi-reps?" Felicia asked maliciously.

"You should not know of such," Cousin Theodora scowled.

"I know that men have their bits of muslin. I wouldn't even be surprised to know that Papa had a ladybird."

"Outrageous!" With surprising strength, she grasped Felicia's shoulders, shook her hard, and pushed her onto the bed.

Taken off balance, Felicia tumbled onto her back.

"You should be whipped, girl! If your father knew what words crossed your lips, he would turn you over his knee. I've a notion to tell him. It would do you a great deal of good!"

"I am twenty-one years old!"

"I am weary of hearing that. I don't care how old you are. You behave like a spoiled brat! What is wrong with you?"

Felicia stood indignantly and walked to the window. "I don't need your interference in my life. That is what is wrong with me!"

"Your father disagrees," Cousin Theodora said smugly. "I would dearly love to wash my hands of you and go back to my home in the country, but I see my duty. You are the most headstrong, impudent little hoyden I have ever seen, but I shall break you. Never fear!"

"You will not!" Felicia shouted. "I will not become the insipid, silly laughingstock that you desire! I won't go to the Allerton ball, and you can't make me!"

"You will go, and you will wear this dress." She held up an offensive, ruffled white gown.

"I'll tear it up first!"

"You would not dare! Your father . . ."

"Ladies!" The duke flung open Felicia's bedroom door. "Cease this brangling! I can hear you all the way down the hall!"

"Father!" Felicia whirled to face him. "Father, please. You must listen!"

"I will not listen to a gel who is talking at the top of her lungs!"

"Father." She lowered her voice. "No doubt Cousin Theodora means well, but we simply cannot get along together."

The duke frowned. "Theodora, allow me to speak with my daughter alone."

Sighing pitifully, the spinster nodded and left.

Felicia's heart leaped. Perhaps, at long last, he was prepared to listen to her! She must remain calm and use good logic.

The duke sat down in the window seat and drew her down beside him.

"Daughter, you have been against Cousin Theodora even before you first laid eyes on her. I know you have sweetness in abundance. Where has it been? You have done nothing but quarrel since she set foot in this house!"

"I dislike her. I dislike having anyone forced on me! Her sense of fashion is ridiculous, and the way she expects me to behave is worse still."

"You do lack modesty, you know."

"Very well then. I shall be modest! Just send her home. Please, Father."

"And the cut of some of your gowns has been a bit extreme."

"I shall throw out whatever you don't like!"

"I wish I could believe all that. I don't wish you to be unhappy, Felicia. I simply want you to become more of an amiable lady."

"I shall!"

"Some spirit in a woman is well and good. Enjoyable, actually. But you do carry it to excess. A man wants a wife who is sweet and malleable. Predictable, if you will!"

"Like the odious Lady Penelope," Felicia said with distaste.

"Her conduct is beyond reproach, is it not?"

"I could never be such a bore! And I might point out that that brainless, little ninnyhammer has not caught herself a husband!"

"She seems to have captured Lord Carlington's interest."

She set her jaw. "Who would want it?"

"They seemed to have attracted a great deal of your attention at the opera."

She looked at him quickly, scarcely believing that he had noticed. "I was merely amusing myself. Father, let us return to the subject of our discussion, which is Cousin Theodora. Please send her home. I promise that I will be everything you wish for! Just give me a chance!"

He smiled thoughtfully. "I will agree to part of it. I will send Theodora home, but first you must prove to me that you have learned your lesson. You will be pleasantly obedient to your cousin's wishes and advice. No more quarreling! You will do as she says, and you will comport yourself with dignity in public. When I see that this is done, I will send Theodora home."

"But, Father, the clothes she wishes me to wear!"

"You shall wear them."

"It is impossible!"

"Felicia . . ."

She hung her head. "Very well, but you will see. I will become a laughingstock, and then no man will have me."

"Just mind my wishes, daughter, or *you* will see that I will resort to stronger measures. I am tired of this house being in a turmoil. And I mean for it to stop at once!"

He kissed her on the forehead and took his leave. She gazed after him. He had made her a bargain. It would be very difficult to carry out, but it seemed to be the only way she could rid herself of this torment. Perhaps she wouldn't look as horrible as she visualized.

That evening, Felicia looked despondently at her reflection in the mirror. She looked like a very prudish schoolgirl, not the fashionable young lady she used to be. The white dress with its fussy embellishments and its high, prim neckline was anything but a ball dress. Her hair, confined in its tight knot, was decidedly puritanical. Her shoes could certainly wreak havoc on a gentleman's shins, and that was just what she wished she could use them for, to kick a certain gentleman swift and hard.

This was Lord Carlington's fault. If it hadn't been for him, Cousin Theodora would be at home and Felicia would be enjoying life as usual. The interfering, arrogant scoundrel! Oh yes, she would get even with him! She would do it just as soon as she could think of a way.

Perhaps she could ruin his romance with his dear, perfectly behaved Lady Penelope. She wouldn't mind getting back at that model of female virtue either. The girl had always treated her with condescension. To think that her father had actually compared her unfavorably to that namby-pamby! It was beyond all belief.

"Well, don't we look pretty!" Cousin Theodora cried, entering the room. "You shall be the most desirable young lady at the Allerton ball!"

Felicia forced a smile. She had gone to great pains to be kind to the woman. She wondered how long she would have to do so.

"Let's be on our way. Your father is waiting!"

"Yes, ma'am, if we must."

"A little nervousness? Don't concern yourself. Everything will be fine!"

"I hope so." Felicia took one more glance at her image and then tried to forget it. People were going to laugh and laugh.

8

T HE BALL HAD begun by the time that the
Favoringham party arrived. Lord Favoringham took himself off to the card room, while Felicia and Cousin Theodora found a seat well out of
the way of the activities. Felicia prepared herself to
be a wallflower.

Several people had noticed them when they had
entered the Allerton mansion, and had hurriedly
hidden laughter behind fluttering fans and clear-
ing of throats. Slowly, they spread the word, whispering from person to person. Soon all eyes in the
room were glancing in the direction of the drab
old spinster and her young counterpart. Felicia
could almost read their thoughts. Could that be
Felicia Harding? What was she up to now?

Her courage vanished and misery took its place.
She, who had always enjoyed a good laugh and
reveled in the ridiculousness of others, was now
the butt of sport for the *ton*. She didn't like it; she
didn't like it a bit.

"Cousin Theodora," she whispered, "may we
leave? I am getting a fearful headache."

"But we have only just arrived! And it is so
pleasant watching the dancing!" Theodora's thin
cheeks were almost pink with excitement. "I'm

sure it is nervousness. You will forget all about it when the young men notice you and begin to ask for dances."

"I don't believe they will."

"Nonsense! You are the prettiest gel here!"

Felicia sighed, watching the couples take the floor for a country dance. She saw with bitterness that even Penelope Hampstead had a partner. This was truly beyond all reason. She looked so horrible that even that odious girl was more in demand.

The next dance was a waltz, and again she sat unclaimed while even the unpopular girls were swung around the room. The waltz was her favorite dance, the one she was most talented at executing. Everyone knew that, but no one wished to dance with such an antidote.

If she were a man, she would call out Lord Carlington and hopefully put a bullet through his heart. If it hadn't been for him, she would be dancing at this moment, her father would be doting on her, and she would be enjoying herself. But as much as she would like to fling it all in his face, she was glad that he was not here to witness her disgrace. He had won a major battle over her, and she did not wish to see him gloat.

"I have heard of the waltz," Cousin Theodora proclaimed, "and I see that it is just as disreputable as I thought. It is nothing but an excuse to engage in improper embraces. There are several very pretty young ladies whose parents must agree, for they are sitting it out."

"They are only beginning their First Season," Felicia explained. "One must receive permission from the patronesses of Almack's before one may waltz. They will be dancing it before long."

"Shocking!" She lifted her lorgnette to peer

more closely. "I cannot conceive why any woman would wish to be held by a man, in such a fashion, in public."

As Cousin Theodora began to launch into a discourse on proper behavior, Felicia put a hand to her forehead. "I'm so sorry, ma'am," she said pitifully, "but I must leave. My head is bursting!"

The woman frowned, then brightened. "I know just the thing! I have some headache powders in my reticule." She hopped up with amazing agility and drew Felicia after her to the ladies' retiring room. Sending the maid for a glass of water, she mixed the draught and poked it toward her cousin. "Drink this. You'll be better in no time!"

Felicia dutifully held her nose and drained the glass.

"Now lie down here. I'll be back to see about you soon. In the meantime, I shall observe the festivities."

"Please take your time," Felicia begged. "When I have a headache such as this, it often takes me a very long while to rid myself of it." With a soft moan, she lay back on the couch and closed her eyes, determined to spend the rest of the ball right where she was.

Felicia knew that dozing would make her pretended illness more effective and the time pass more quickly, but her thoughts were too disordered to allow the slightest bit of relaxation. She would never leave the house again, so long as she had to wear these horrible clothes. Her father was asking the impossible. Didn't he realize how ridiculous she appeared? Didn't he even care?

She could not go through an evening like this again. Even Lady Penelope was probably laughing! By tomorrow morning, Felicia would be the talk of the town. Ladies would giggle in their drawing rooms, and men would laugh in their clubs. She hoped they would make sport of her father as well. This was as much his fault as Lord Carlington's. Men! How odious they could be!

Lord Favoringham's challenge to her was impossible. It could not be met. She would not allow herself be placed in such an embarrassing situation again. She would approach her father in the morning and demand that she be permitted to return to the country. Her reputation must surely be in shreds, but if she left London immediately the *ton* might forget by next year.

But why wait until tomorrow? Why let anyone else see her in this deplorable state? She would slip away home now and pack.

Rising, Felicia left the ladies' room and made her way quietly to the coat room in the downstairs hall. But before she could request her wrap and carriage, the servants' attention was focused on the arrival of none other than the Earl of Carlington. He was splendidly dressed as usual, in faultless black evening attire and a many-caped cloak lined with shimmering blue satin. A footman removed his outer wrap with a flourish and accepted, with awe, His Lordship's hat and gloves.

Felicia's heart gave a lurch. How could a man so arrogant and so despisable be so beautifully handsome? She couldn't keep her eyes off him. He had the looks every young lady dreamed of, and the wealth, and the title. It was too bad that he didn't have the manner as well. Oh, what a terrible waste!

As Lord Carlington turned to go up the stairs his blue eyes caught hers. A look of amusement crossed his face as he proceeded to survey her in entirety. He made his bow.

Felicia's temper flared. How could she stand there half-mesmerized by him! Her disgrace was his fault. If he had not pushed that high, aristocratic nose into Favoringham affairs, none of this would have happened. Now his entrance was cutting short her successful escape. She glared at him.

"My, what have we here?" he asked mildly, approaching. "I didn't know this was a masquerade."

Her hand ached to slap his face. "It is not, my lord," she said tightly. "This has become my normal attire since you decided to interfere in my life. It is your fault that I am forced to wear these clothes!"

"I hardly think that." He bit back a grin. "I am neither a modiste nor a hairdresser."

Felicia drew back to strike him, but Lord Carlington easily parried her blow and caught her wrist, tucking her hand neatly in his arm. "My dear, in front of the servants?"

"Let me go!" she demanded.

"Not until you tell me what all this is about." He drew her aside into a small alcove.

"This is most improper," she said irritably.

"Now, now. You were going to hit me. At least I deserve to know the reason why."

"It is because you have used me in a most disgusting manner!"

He laughed. "If I had 'used' you, minx, I don't think you would have found it disgusting."

"Oh!" she cried with outrage. "You are the most despisable, odious man . . ."

"I know, I know. You've said it all before. Now won't you tell me why you are here at the Allerton ball, all dressed up like a schoolgirl? And not a very pretty one at that, I might add."

"You have caused it! If you had not complained

to my father of my behavior, he would never have thought of sending for Cousin Theodora. It is her idea that I dress this way and behave like a simpleton, too! Everyone is laughing!"

"I shouldn't be surprised." He chuckled.

"Indeed! Why should you care that I am miserable because of you?" Feeling herself very nearly on the brink of tears, she pulled free of him. "I am leaving!"

"But the Allertons always have a very nice event."

"Enjoy it!" she hissed, hurrying to a nearby servant. "My wrap, please, and my carriage."

Lord Carlington followed her, leaning down to whisper in her ear. "It is all well and good to laugh at others, but it is quite different when the shoe is on the other foot. Is that not so, Lady Felicia?"

She swelled with anger. "How dare you accuse me of being a poor sport? If you possessed a modicum of feelings for others you would know that this has gone far beyond a laughing matter!"

"On the contrary, I have a great deal of feeling for others, as witnessed by my support of various social programs."

"Fustian!"

"Good evening, my lady." Lord Carlington bowed and started up the stairs.

She glared at his retreating back. Damn him! How could he accuse her of poor sportsmanship, when anyone could see that this was not a joke, but a disaster? He didn't care what he had caused! He had ruined her life, and it didn't matter at all to him. A feeling for others? Ha! She would fix him!

"Your wrap, m'lady."

"I'm staying!" She thrust her cloak back into the

servant's hands and, narrowing her eyes, went up the steps behind the earl. She caught up with him after he had greeted his host and hostess and started into the main ballroom. "I have decided not to deprive you of my company," she said coyly. "Please save me your first waltz, and the supper dance, of course!"

He stiffened and stared at her as though she had lost her mind. "Are you asking . . ."

"Oh yes, my lord. Is there something wrong with that?"

He eyed her warily. "As we both know, Lady Felicia, the gentleman usually does the asking."

"In my case, I am sure we may make an exception. Or are you ashamed to be seen with me?"

"I am not so unkind."

"Good!" Felicia flashed a glance around the room and saw with satisfaction that Lady Penelope had witnessed their entrance together. A brief look of dismay crossed the girl's face before it was replaced with her usual bland expression. Felicia wondered if Lord Carlington had noticed. Gazing up into his face, she saw him looking down at her. That was all the better. She smiled coquettishly.

"You are a baggage."

"What a thing to say, my lord!"

"It was a devilish day when I made your acquaintance."

"I agree wholeheartedly!"

"And I am not so fool enough not to realize that you are up to something."

"Indeed?" She dimpled.

"First you try to hit me, now you are flirting with me. Wouldn't that give any man cause to wonder?"

"Probably, but the orchestra is, this moment, striking up our waltz. Shall we?"

"Perhaps you would like to lead as well!"

"No, I shall leave that to you," she said airily, "if you are capable?"

"Of course I am capable!" He caught her waist and swung her expertly onto the floor.

Immediately, Felicia realized that she had made a mistake. She had meant to embarrass him through his seeming choice of such a dowdy female for a partner, and she had intended to cause trouble between him and Lady Penelope. Now all that was suddenly forgotten.

She loved to waltz, and Lord Carlington was such a proficient dancer that her anger cooled and pleasure took its place. Dancing with him was like dancing on air. She had planned to move awkwardly in his arms, but it was impossible. Yielding, she let him sweep her around the ballroom and quite forgot her ridiculous clothing.

As if he felt her soften, he drew her closer. "You are an exquisite dancer, Lady Felicia."

"I enjoy it very much," she answered honestly, lifting her head to meet his quizzical eyes. "Surprised, my lord?"

"A little."

"What did you expect?"

"Truthfully, I expected you to use the occasion to grind my toes and kick my shins."

Her irritation returned. "I am sorry to cause you disappointment." Deliberately, she trod on his foot.

"Can't you be a good girl?"

"Not where you are concerned! Also, I am not a girl, I am a woman."

He laughed lightly. "For once I find I must agree with you. I am very much aware that you are a woman."

She caught her breath, her pulse racing. "You are provoking."

"Oh? No longer odious and despisable?"

"You are that, too! And you are holding me too closely."

He did not slacken his embrace. "But you are such a delicious armful."

"My lord!"

Lord Carlington had turned the tables on her. He must be aware that he had made her slightly dizzy and breathless. Her knees were quickly turning to water when the dance ended and she managed to make her curtsy.

He bowed. "Despite your bristles, Lady Felicia, I have enjoyed our waltz. May I escort you to your chaperon?"

She nodded. "You must be anxious to see that paragon of virtue that you have caused me to put up with."

"To be sure."

Felicia directed him toward where she had sat with Cousin Theodora. With sinking heart she saw the spinster standing rigidly before her chair, her face a mask of disapproval. "Oh, dear." Squaring her shoulders, she forced a smile. "Cousin Theodora, may I present Lord Carlington? Sir, my cousin."

"Madam," he bowed.

"My lord. I am honored, but you must excuse us." Abruptly, she caught Felicia's arm and jerked her forward.

The earl frowned. "I shall look forward to our supper dance, Lady Felicia."

"I'm sorry, my lord," Cousin Theodora said in a strained voice. "Lady Felicia will not be in attendance." Without further ado, she rounded on her charge. "How can you be so thoughtless of your reputation! Waltzing! Young ladies do not waltz!"

"Cousin . . ." Felicia began, feeling her cheeks burn.

"I shall fetch your father from the card room, and we will go home at once. This time you will be punished! I am sure that the duke will agree. There will be no more dancing, until you learn to conduct yourself properly."

"But I have received permission to waltz from the patronesses of Almack's."

"You have not received my permission!"

Felicia lifted her chin and bit back tears of frustration. "Yes, ma'am." In a blur, she left the ballroom with her detestable cousin.

Shannon watched the scene with horror. When he had pompously suggested to Lord Favoringham that his daughter needed a companion, he had never dreamed of anything like this. How could the duke believe that this old harridan was suitable for Felicia? The chit needed a lady who would guide her with patience and understanding. This cousin would either make her more rebellious, or break her spirit entirely.

He took a glass of champagne from the tray of a passing waiter and strolled out onto the balcony. It was no wonder that Felicia was so overset, nor that she blamed him. When he had first seen her on the stairs, clad in that horrible dress, he had assumed that she had concocted a prank designed to get even with him. But it was no joke. The ugly termagant had trigged her out as an unfashionable schoolgirl, and her father had to have condoned it. Pretty, lively Felicia had completely disappeared under the furbelows and skinned-back hair, and she was very unhappy.

It was all his fault. He had no business sticking his nose into the affairs of Lady Felicia Harding. Looking back, he couldn't understand why he had done it, except that she was such a challenge. He had wanted to give her a setdown, but he hadn't wanted to make her miserable.

Briefly he thought of talking again with Lord Favoringham, and quickly dismissed the notion from his mind. It was bad enough that he had ventured his opinion in the first place. To continue to interfere would be the height of impropriety and impertinence. There was a time when he might have risked it anyway, but those days were past.

He turned back to the ballroom but the company had palled. Making his way discreetly around the outer edge of the crowd, he took his leave of Allerton House. Perhaps in the congenial atmosphere of his club, he could forget the damage he had done to the lady. It was, after all, none of his affair. Fiery little Felicia would have to find her own way to cope with what had happened. Only when his carriage drew away from the curb did he remember, with mortification, that he had completely ignored Lady Penelope.

9

THE CARRIAGE RIDE to Favoringham House was silent, but in the dim light from the lanterns, Felicia could see her cousin's lips pressed forcefully together and knew that she had not heard the last of what Cousin Theodora considered improper conduct. Her head was truly aching now. She hoped that the woman would wait until the next day before enacting her scene.

The evening had already been as much as she could bear. Her emotions had run the gamut from mortification, to anger, and then to that strange feeling she had experienced when she had danced with Lord Carlington. It was almost as if she were drawn to him. She remembered that her friend, Barbara, had said he was attracted to her. Could it be that she was attracted to him as well? But that was impossible. She hated Lord Carlington. He was the cause of all her troubles. Yet they had danced so beautifully together . . .

She lay her throbbing head against the squabs and closed her eyes. It was all too much to think about. First, of course, she must gather her wits for combat with Cousin Theodora. Next she must persuade her father to permit her to go home to the country. Only then could she possibly begin to sort out her feelings about the handsome earl. If only it could wait until tomorrow!

But it was not to be. Cousin Theodora marshaled Felicia and her father into the drawing room and firmly shut the door, standing before it as if to prevent anyone's escape. Impatiently, the duke took himself to the sideboard and poured himself a hefty glass of brandy. Grimly, Felicia collapsed into a winged chair by the hearth, and waited for the storm to break.

"Well?" her father asked. "What is it now?"

The gates burst. "I have never been so shocked in all my life!" cried Cousin Theodora. "Such fast behavior! And I thought I had made progress in the last day or so!"

"As I explained," Felicia defended, "there was nothing wrong with my conduct at all! It was perfectly proper."

Disgruntled that their abrupt departure from the ball had drawn him away from a winning hand of whist, Lord Favoringham frowned at both of them. "May we not discuss this in the morning?"

Happy to hear this, and recognizing the signs of his rising temper, his daughter readily agreed, but his cousin did not. The spinster violently shook her head and wrung her hands. "It is a situation which should be resolved at once, Your Grace. What if that . . . that *man* should have the audacity to call tomorrow, before we have talked? After the girl's lustful behavior toward him, I should not be surprised. He will expect further favors!"

"What man?"

Her cousin glared at her. "Speak, girl!"

"It was Lord Carlington, Father. I danced a waltz with him."

He chuckled. "So the earl found he was not immune to your charms, my dear?"

Felicia, not about to admit to her truly forward behavior, shrugged. "Perhaps."

"It was perfectly improper! There she was, in that man's arms, with him whispering in her ear as though she were a strumpet! I have never seen such an indecent display from a well-bred young lady, or from a so-called gentleman for that matter!"

"Everyone waltzes if they have received permission from the patronesses of Almack's," Felicia protested. "Father, you know that!"

"It is disgusting! A proper gentleman would not even embrace his wife like that in public! That man may be a gentleman by birth, but not in truth! He is exactly the type of cad Felicia must be protected from."

The duke threw up his hands. "Stop it, both of you!" He took a deep breath. "Cousin Theodora, I assure you that Lord Carlington is a fine gentleman. Even in his younger days, he would never have taken liberties with a young lady of quality."

Theodora knitted her lips. "I have never known a man, even a gentleman, to refuse liberties when they were offered."

He shook his head. "Felicia, did you, perhaps, dance too closely to the earl?"

"I certainly did not! It was most circumspect."

"Are you sure?"

"Yes I am sure!" Felicia flung herself to her feet and began to pace the room. "Father, this has gone far enough! Our bargain is impossible. How can I exhibit proper behavior to you, when she continues to feed you these untruths? Her ideas are outdated, and so is her view of fashion. Look at me! I was a laughingstock tonight because of these horrible clothes! No one wished to be near me, let alone dance with me. If I have to wear these dresses, I will never set foot outside of this house again!"

"You were attractive enough for that man to ask you to dance!" Theodora snapped.

"Lord Carlington danced with me because I asked him to!" Felicia blurted.

Her cousin's shocked outburst was silenced by her father's roar. "Felicia!"

She bit her lip, wishing that she had never been goaded into making such an admission. If Lord Carlington held his tongue, no one ever would have known. Now, through her own folly, she had admitted it and must suffer the consequences.

"Lord help us all," Cousin Theodora mumbled, waving her vinaigrette under her nose.

"How could you do such a thing?" Lord Favoringham cried. "Even at your most outrageous, you have never performed such a breach of simple conduct."

"I was angry with him. I blame him for all of this! I was perfectly happy before he became involved."

The duke drank deeply and refilled his glass. "It is not his fault, Felicia. When you entered Carlington's house, you gave him no choice but to become involved."

"Entered Lord Carlington's house!" cried Cousin Theodora. "He has compromised her?"

"No!" Felicia said savagely. "It was not like that."

"He must marry her. Your Grace, you must insist upon immediate betrothal!"

"I won't marry him!"

"Ladies!" Lord Favoringham shouted. "The earl is innocent of wrongdoing. I shall certainly not accuse him of compromising my daughter, Theodora, so get that out of your head! He didn't ask for what happened, and through it all, he acted as a proper gentleman. Good God, I'd never trap a fellow man in such a shabby way! And there's an end to it!"

Cousin Theodora made a huff of disgust and eyed Felicia with heavy-browed disapproval. "And what, young lady, were you doing at Lord Carlington's house?"

"Enough of that!" the duke interjected. "It is this present situation which concerns me."

"Indeed," agreed his tight-lipped cousin. "So what are we to do?"

"First of all, we'll hope Carlington keeps his mouth shut about it. I believe he will. I have heard no mention of our other little scandal that concerned him. The earl is a man of honor."

"He is a nosy busybody," Felicia said waspishly.

"Daughter, if you think so ill of the man, I wonder why you even spoke to him tonight."

"Revenge, Father. Pure revenge. I wanted to embarrass him by having everyone see him in the company of such a hideous dowd. And I wanted to cause him trouble with that insipid little dolt, Penelope Hampstead, whom he dotes on."

The duke started to chuckle, thought better of it, and smothered it in his brandy glass. "I think it would be wise if we retired for the night. We'll talk of this tomorrow and, perhaps, come up with further solutions."

"I have one right now," his daughter announced. "I want to go home to the country. Just as soon as possible."

Cousin Theodora studied her thoughtfully. "It might be wise," she agreed, "until all of this blows over."

Felicia looked at her hopefully. Could her odious cousin actually join with her in gaining the duke's approval? Perhaps Cousin Theodora had actually become fed up with the situation, and wished to give up and return to her home.

"I shall, of course, go with her," the spinster continued. "In the rural atmosphere, I may instruct her without diversion. When we return to London, Felicia will be a properly behaved young lady."

"I want to be alone, Father, to mull this over! I cannot get my thoughts in order if I must be subjected to Cousin Theodora's 'lady lessons.' "

"Felicia? Cousin Theodora? What you have suggested just may be the best idea, but we will not go into it now. As I said, we'll discuss this matter tomorrow. I've had enough of it for tonight!" the duke decided.

"Yes, Father." She dutifully kissed him, and hurried from the room and up the stairs before Cousin Theodora could catch up to her and open the subject again. Darting into her room, she turned the key in the lock, surprising her dozing abigail. "Don't open this for anyone, Mary. If I see that woman again tonight, I'll murder her!"

The abigail's eyes were full of questions, but she silently helped her mistress out of her gown and into her nightrail.

Felicia dismissed her and cuddled herself under the covers. After the loud voices, the London night seemed very quiet, with only an occasional carriage clipping along in the streets. The pain in her head eased.

It seemed that nothing she could come up with would rid her of Cousin Theodora. Even an escape to the country would be ruined by the lady's presence. Was there nothing she could do?

Tomorrow she would have to face her father again. She would beg and plead, and probably get nowhere with him. He was convinced that Cousin Theodora was of some benefit to her.

Drowsily, she let her mind drift back to the ball. Alone in her bed, it was easy to admit that it had been heavenly dancing in Lord Carlington's arms. He hadn't been stuffy at all. In fact, he had been rather teasing and flirtatious, despite his moments of irritation. She had been right when she had stated that he would be improved immensely by a shock. Unfortunately, he would get no such thing from Lady Penelope.

Felicia ground her teeth. She hated Penelope Hampstead. That young lady had all the luck. She would never be upbraided for misbehavior, for she would never set a foot outside the ordinary. That must be what it took to gain the admiration of such as Lord Carlington. Well, if that was what he wanted, he was welcome to it, and she hoped that he would spend the rest of his life in utter boredom.

Once inside the hallowed sanctum of White's on St. James Street, Shannon had scarcely greeted several acquaintances before being hailed by his old friends Marcus Grassham, Tom Garland, and Ev Halloran. He had avoided the trio since the fateful incident in the square, but tonight it was to be impossible. Suddenly he didn't care. Their spirited company might take his mind off Felicia Harding and the trouble he had caused her, but he would take care not to become involved in any of their outlandish activities. He joined them, requesting a bottle of port from the hovering waiter.

"What? No brandy, Shan?" Lord Grassham commented. "Part of the 'Impeccable Gentleman Plan,' no doubt!"

Shannon rolled his eyes toward the ceiling and awaited the onslaught.

"Haven't seen you in awhile." Tom grinned. "Thought you might be getting married."

"Yes," Ev chuckled. "We saw the ad in the paper."

Shannon raised an eyebrow. "Saw it? Or placed it?"

"Now Shan, you know us better than that!"

"I thought I did," he said with mock seriousness, "but, alas, I've been unable to determine which of you had the idea in the first place. Each of you is perfectly capable, of course."

"You are blaming us?" Marcus asked with incredulity. "Damme! Gentlemen, shall we be forced to call out our friend?"

"I fear we must," Tom said sadly. "All three of us at once should not be too much for a great war hero. Choose your weapon, Shan!"

"All three of you at one time?"

"All or none!"

"Well then . . ." He paused, studying them. "Since I cannot fire three pistols at once, or hold three swords, I'll choose women. A squareful of women! Write your wills, for you'll never get out of that one alive!"

"It could be a pleasant way to die," Ev murmured.

"Trust me, it wouldn't!"

They laughed. "We must bow to your experience, Shan!"

"But as you see, I escaped."

"A triumph of superior military strategy?"

"No," he said sardonically. "I ran."

The waiter served Shannon's port and went off to fetch more brandy for the other gentlemen. The earl swirled the wine in his glass and took a sip, noting the look of expectancy in his friends' eyes.

"Since your view from Tom's house was rather limited, I'm sure you're dying of curiosity to know what went on when the ladies stormed the portals." He held up his hand. "Don't deny it. I saw the three of you at the window, laughing your heads off."

"Caught again!"

"Indeed." Shannon nodded. "When that bevy of beauties burst through the door, my servants sprang to arms. Hearing the disturbance, I went into the hall, took one look, and fled. I barricaded myself in my room, and hid until the war was over. That, gentleman, is the story of the Battle of Carlington House!"

"And you didn't even interview a single one of the candidates?" Tom asked with disappointment.

"None."

The Earl of Grassham looked at him thoughtfully, mulling the brandy in his mouth before swallowing. "Then who was the young lady we saw you leaving with later in the morning? We thought she might have been a successful applicant."

Shannon's heart leaped to his throat. Why hadn't he realized that his friends would be keeping a close scrutiny on the house? He should have dressed Lady Felicia as a servant, and sent her and her abigail on their way. Instead he had become so incensed with her, that he must deliver her in person to her father to assure himself that she would be found out and receive a scold. His stupidity had gained nothing but trouble for her, and now for him as well. It could be a fatal error.

"I don't know what you're talking about, Marcus," he said with a coolness he was far from feeling.

"We saw you leave in your carriage, accompanying a young lady and, if I may not be mistaken, her chaperon."

"Yes we did, Shan," seconded Tom.

"Oh, *that* young lady." Shannon quickly marshaled his thoughts. "That was quite unfortunate. You see, the lady was going on a visit to a friend's house. She became caught up in the mob and took refuge in my mews. My coachman brought it to my attention and, when it was safe, I escorted her home. You should think about the innocent when you construct your schemes!" he finished severely.

"Not an applicant then."

"Certainly not! In fact, she was quite overset about the whole thing. Can't say that I blame her!"

"Failed to see the humor, eh?"

Shannon didn't like the look of speculation on Grassham's face. The earl didn't believe him. Despite his superficiality, his friend had always had an uncanny ability to recognize when someone was lying to him.

"Who was she, Shan?" Marcus asked lightly.

He pretended to consider. "I can't remember. She wasn't very attractive. I fear I took no note of her!"

"A pity. Might have been interesting! Where does she live?"

"I don't remember."

"You said you took her home."

"Yes I did, but I took little heed." He drank deep of the port. "It was of no importance."

"I suppose not." Marcus smiled knowingly.

"Well, now that we've exhausted that subject, how about a game of cards?"

Shannon thankfully agreed. He would be congenial, but he'd stay as short a time as possible. If he knew his friends, the subject was far from ended.

When the Earl of Carlington took his leave, his friends got their heads together immediately.

"He seemed glad to see us at first," Tom commented, "but then he grew anxious to be away."

"I suppose we'll have to admit that he just doesn't enjoy our company anymore."

"That's not it at all." Marcus shook his head. "He's hiding something. Didn't you see it?"

"No."

"He was having a good time until I mentioned that young lady. Shan's memory is just as good as anyone else's, better than most. He knows damn good and well who that young lady is, and he knows where she lives."

"Maybe she's his ladybird."

"I don't think so. Why should he hide that? And if she were, he wouldn't bring her to his house. Even if he did, she wouldn't have her maid with her!"

"Compromised," Tom said darkly. "She's a lady of quality."

"Exactly!"

"Well, we'd better stay out of it. We didn't mean for that to happen."

The earl drummed his fingers on the table. "Wouldn't it be amusing to find out her identity?"

"Yes, but . . ."

"I'd bet a monkey that I'd recognize her again. She seemed vaguely familiar. I've seen her somewhere before."

"Shan would kill us!"

"Oh, if we search it out, we'll not let the cat out of the bag." Marcus smiled with anticipation. "Besides, gentlemen, have we anything better to do with our time?"

10

IN THE MORNING, Felicia presented herself early at breakfast, hoping to talk with her father before Cousin Theodora poisoned his thoughts once again. It was all in vain. According to Andrew, who had surprisingly turned up for the meal, the duke had left the house half an hour before.

"Damme!" She had no difficulty deciding why Lord Favoringham had taken himself off so early. He wanted to avoid the inevitable confrontation and decision. He would put it off as long as possible in hopes that people would change their minds, tempers would cool, and things would return to normal.

That wasn't going to happen. Things had not been routine at Favoringham House ever since Cousin Theodora had come. They would not return to normal until she left. That included Felicia's going to the country. If she were forced to take Cousin Theodora with her, she would refuse to go. Here in London at least, her father would have a portion of her discomfort.

She helped herself to a generous serving from the buffet of breakfast offerings, and sat down disgruntledly. "That is just like him. He is avoiding the issue."

"Something wrong?" Andrew asked.

"How can you put it so mildly?" she flared. "Everything is wrong! Isn't that why you have made yourself scarce?"

"I'd just as soon steer a clear path away from Cousin Theodora."

"Fine! You're allowed it. But not me! Can you imagine how I looked at the Allerton ball last night?" She bitterly stabbed her fork into her eggs. "I was a laughingstock! No one would dance with me."

"Carlington did."

Felicia looked at him with surprise. Perhaps Lord Carlington had gone about spreading his side of the story! Panic knotted her stomach. "How do you know about that?"

"Father told me."

She exhaled a pent-up breath. "If he told you that, I'm sure he also told you that *I* was the one who asked *him* to dance. It was wrong of me, of course, but ... I was angry. Drew, I am at the end of my rope. I cannot bear it any longer."

"Perhaps it would be easier to go along with it."

"I can't!" she cried. "You don't know what it's like! Day in and day out, I must listen to Cousin Theodora's prosings on how to be a proper lady. I must wear these ridiculous dresses. And, if that were not enough, I must actually wear them into Society and make a fool of myself!" She burst into tears.

"Good God, 'Licia!" Andrew stared at her with horror.

"Don't mind it," she sobbed. "I'll be all right in a moment."

"I have never seen you so overset. Dammit all, I don't think I've ever seen you cry!"

Felicia wiped her eyes and blew her nose into her napkin. "I'm all right now," she gurgled.

"Something must be done."

"I wanted to go to the country. My reputation must surely be in shreds. If I went away until next year, people might forget."

"An excellent idea."

"But Cousin Theodora has decided that she should come with me. She says that in the country without interruptions, she may have more influence on me." She sniffled. "I can't bear it, Andrew!"

"Of course not. We must think of something."

"But what? Father is avoiding the issue. To me, that means that he is not ready to dismiss Cousin Theodora."

"True."

She eyed her brother levelly, a thought forming in her mind. "You could take me to the country, Drew. I'll run away. And when Father discovers it, perhaps he'll realize how serious I am about ridding myself of that woman!"

"I!"

"Who else? I would not want to take a common stage. I wouldn't know how to go about it. But you could take me."

"Father would have me drawn and quartered!"

"We could keep it secret."

"He would still find out! Some servant would tell him. I'm sorry, Felicia, it's out of the question. Why, he might even shut off my allowance!"

"You know that Father never stays angry for very long. Besides, you could come to the country and keep me company until he relented."

"I don't want to go to the country. I'm having a good time here."

"Thank you, Andrew," she said stiffly. "You are a great help."

He flushed. "See here, Felicia, you'd better do as Father says. You're in enough trouble already. Lay back and see what happens next." Shaking his head, he stood. "I'm sorry, I just can't do anything more." With an unhappy sigh, he left the breakfast room.

When Shannon presented himself at Favoringham House, he was not surprised to find the salon empty of callers. In the past, before he had meddled in her life, Lady Felicia must have had admirers. She was so pretty, and so full of high spirits, she must have been overwhelmed with suitors. But the *ton* was fickle. Once someone had set themselves up to be outlandish, Society could quickly take them in disfavor. After last night, even though he had danced with her, she was probably ruined. Invitations would drop off and finally cease altogether. Her voucher to Almack's would be withdrawn. There would be nothing for her to do but return to the country and marry some hard-drinking country squire, who would consider her nothing but a broodmare, and who would exhibit more interest in his hounds and horses than in his wife. Lady Felicia would wither away, bearing children every year, and catering to her boisterous spouse and his red-faced friends. It would all be his fault.

He sat down beside the fire and slowly sipped the glass of excellent sherry that Favoringham's officious butler had served him. He must think of something to do. The young lady could not be sentenced to such a dismal fate.

"You shall not see that man!" The strident voice in the hall pierced through the walls and door.

"Oh, yes I shall!"

"I won't permit it! Stop her, Murray!"

The door burst open and Lady Felicia, pink-cheeked with exertion, hurled herself through it, her cousin clasping her elbow. Behind was a phalanx of footmen, glancing helplessly from one to the other, and the once-dignified butler, who had lost his aplomb and was waving his hands frantically.

Shannon looked on in disbelief. Lady Felicia herself had not come through the onslaught unscathed. Her high-necked, long-sleeved, Quaker-gray dress was in disarray. A golden lock, pulled loose from her severe chignon, hung down the side of her face as though someone had tried to catch her by the hair. She had lost a shoe in the scuffle, and her dainty stockinged foot protruded slightly from beneath her hem.

"Take her to her room!" Cousin Theodora cried. "Must I remind you that I have the authority to discipline?"

The servants exchanged fearful looks. Finally, with a great drawing of breath, the butler and the largest footman came forward.

"Don't touch her," Shannon heard himself say with cold, measured tones.

They fell back with relief. Here was the real voice of authority. He was an aristocratic peer, a war hero, and, thank God, a man. Even Cousin Theodora relaxed her hold, surprise written on her thin face.

Lady Felicia seized the opportunity to escape. She quickly walked across the room to stand by the fire, placing Shannon between herself and her tormentors.

"Leave us," the earl ordered, feeling all the nobility of his powerful medieval ancestors.

The servants, falling back on their own obedient forebearers, gratefully withdrew.

"You, too, madam."

Cousin Theodora carried the scene back to the present. "It isn't proper, my lord."

"You may leave the door open."

"I do not think . . ."

"Madam, I did not come here to fence with you," Shannon said in his most threatening voice. "I assure you that I will conduct myself with perfect propriety. Now go."

She brought herself up to her full height. "I have never trusted a man's assurances. I have always found them to be deceitful."

"You cannot have been around very many men." He took a stride forward. "I believe that you hate and fear them, which is why you are an aging spinster and the reason you are attempting to turn Lady Felicia into a dowdy old antidote like yourself. I shall not allow it."

"You . . . shall . . ." Cousin Theodora was forced to tilt her head to look up at him.

"Get out of here!" he hissed, and the woman fled.

"Bravo!" Felicia giggled. "You made short work of her."

"Not short enough for my taste." He turned to her with a rueful smile. "I've made your life a misery, haven't I?"

"Yes, my lord, you have." She moved past him to the door, shut it, and turned the key in the lock.

"Lady Felicia!"

"I won't have the old biddy eavesdropping," she said briskly. "Now she may have free rein to imagine the worst of orgiastic scenes! I believe that is how she enlivens her life."

Shannon felt a slow blush crawl up his cheeks.

"Have I embarrassed you, my lord?"

"A little."

"Good! It gives me great pleasure. But why do I feel that your profound dignity is not quite what it seems? I have heard that you were a dissolute rake in your younger days, but I never quite believed it. However, upon further acquaintance with you, I have glimpsed traces of unexpected mischief. Your cool facade, Lord Carlington, is hiding something."

His pristine cravat seemed to be choking him. He cleared his throat and reached up to loosen it slightly. "Lady Felicia, I did not come here to discuss myself."

She laughed lightly. "I do so love to stir you up. Have I made you angry?"

"No." As she passed him, going to the window, he caught the sweet, musky odor of *eau de cologne.* No toilette of roses for Lady Felicia! The little minx would wear something very French and teasingly sensual. It was so at odds with her prim gown that it made him want to laugh.

"Well, my lord," she said, clasping her hands behind her and staring out at the street, "if you did not come here to discuss yourself, what did you wish to talk about?"

Shannon's eyes took in her slender waist and her slim, but nicely rounded hips. How could such a delicate form conceal such explosiveness? In bed, she would be . . .

"My lord?"

He took a deep breath, trying to still his thundering heartbeat. "I came to discuss your predicament."

"Feeling guilty?" She turned to face him.

"I suppose I am. I wish to help you."

"There is little you can do."

"You could marry me," he blurted. Shannon seemed in shock from the statement, looking around to see if it had possibly come from a source other than him.

Felicia briefly stared at him, stunned, then began to laugh. "That is perfectly ridiculous! I would merely be exchanging one prison for another."

"I don't think so," he said stubbornly, suddenly wanting to defend himself and his preposterous offer. "You would be rid of your cousin."

"You would be just as provoking, although I do suppose that I could dress more fashionably. This is ridiculous! How can you even consider it, when we cannot spend five minutes in each other's company without quarreling? No, Lord Carlington, it would be a complete disaster." She looked at him through her long eyelashes. "I do believe, however, that it is proper that I should thank you for the honor you have bestowed . . ."

"Don't bother," he interrupted, returning to his seat by the fire. "You may find that you have to marry me." He looked pointedly at the locked door. He was beginning to enjoy this. "This is the second time you've placed me in a compromising situation."

"Oh dear, shall your mother or sister defend your honor by calling me out? Pistols at dawn? Or will it be embroidery needles?"

"Don't joke about it. You may have gone too far this time. I have my own reputation to consider. If I took my offer to your father, what do you think would be the result?"

"The two of you would drag me to the altar." She flounced down into the chair across from him.

"It would almost be worth it. The first thing I would do on our honeymoon would be to turn you over my knee and give you the spanking you so richly deserve."

"My goodness!" Felicia cried with mock fear. "My father would never marry me to a man who professed his intentions to beat his wife!"

Shannon couldn't keep from grinning. "Lady Felicia, I think you will always be a step ahead of me. Will I never win a battle against you?"

"Not if I can help it!"

Shannon shook his head. "May we be serious for a moment?"

"Of course, my lord."

"You went to a great deal of effort to see me today, despite the wishes of your cousin. Why?"

"I might ask the same, although you must admit that the amount of effort you expended was the lesser."

"I have already answered your question: I wish to help you. Now mine?"

She smiled at him candidly. "I think you are the only reasonably sane person in my acquaintance at present. I do enjoy sharpening my wits on you." She looked at him more closely. "Do you really wish to help me?"

"Yes I do."

"Then you may take me to my home in the country."

"What?"

"It isn't very far. I would rent a carriage myself, but the way goes across Hounslow Heath, so I would prefer a proper male escort, especially since I would be traveling at night."

Shannon sighed. "Of course I assume that your father would have no knowledge of this?"

"Never fear, my lord. It is impossible that you would be caught assisting me. We must leave tonight. My father is avoiding me and Cousin

Theodora. He won't be home till the wee hours. My cousin always retires early. I will meet you on the corner at midnight, and we will be at Favoringham Park by morning."

"The servants . . ."

"Papa never requires them to wait up for him."

"Your brother . . ."

"Never comes home till morning! You see? There is nothing to fear. I will leave my father a note so that he will not worry, and all will be well. I'd never tell him of your involvement."

"What do you expect to gain from this?"

"I will gain my freedom from all of them!"

"Lord Favoringham may come after you, or merely send your Cousin Theodora to join you."

"I'll worry about that if it happens. In the meantime, I will be free!"

"And I'll be swinging at Tyburn for kidnapping the Duke of Favoringham's daughter."

"Fustian! At the very worst, you would have to marry me, and you've already made yourself willing to do that. Help me, Lord Carlington!" Felicia turned doe eyes on him. "I shall be eternally grateful. If I ever see you again, I won't even quarrel with you."

"It is against my better judgment."

"But you'll do it?" She bounced anxiously on the edge of her chair. "After all, this is all your fault."

Shannon sighed. "All right, but if we are caught . . ."

"Impossible! By this time tomorrow, I will be free and you will be at your club laughing about how worried you were. It's simple!"

"I have found, Lady Felicia," he said dryly, "that where you are concerned, nothing is ever simple."

* * *

Felicia spent the rest of the day setting the stage for her journey. She decided against letting her abigail in on the secret. Mary was too afraid of being fired, especially now that her mistress had been plunged into disgrace. The maid was also terrified of Cousin Theodora. If she sensed any hint of misconduct in the offing, she would be sure to run to the woman to report what she knew.

This could have made it difficult to pack a few belongings for the trip, for Felicia had never been much in the habit of spending time in her room. Usually when she was there, Mary was in attendance until it was bedtime. Today, however, as punishment for seeing Lord Carlington behind closed doors, Cousin Theodora had confined her to her room. Mary went on about her business, leaving her at her leisure to make her preparations.

Ignoring her horrible new dresses, she packed two of her pretty old ones, and certain necessary cosmetics, into a small portmanteau and hid it under her bed. Then, having the rest of the day and evening before her, she curled up on her window seat with a book.

But she was too excited to read, and Lord Carlington's handsome face kept swimming before her eyes. He was being quite nice in helping her. She realized that he considered himself to have suffered greatly at her hands, and it was really very kind of him to come forward to assist. She would make an effort to be pleasant on the journey and to refrain from quarreling with him.

Dinnertime came and went. With Cousin Theodora's great belief in family members dining together, Felicia thought she might be released from confinement in her chamber to take her meal downstairs. But it was not to be. Promptly at the hour at which supper would be served, Mary brought her a tray. Staring at its meager contents, Felicia was doubly glad that she had decided to escape. Evidently, Cousin Theodora's punishments included starvation as well!

Her boredom increased as the hands of her mantel clock moved slowly toward twelve. Cousin Theodora arrived for a brief lecture on duty and proper conduct, then bid her good night. She rang for Mary.

"I believe I shall retire. I am bored stiff."

The maid nodded sympathetically, as she assisted Felicia in getting ready for bed. "Soon it will be tomorrow, my lady, and the punishment will all be over."

"Yes it will. Not long at all." Felicia smiled and got into bed. "Good night."

"Sleep well, my lady."

When the clock struck eleven, Felicia leaped from bed and began to dress in her attractive, deep-blue traveling ensemble. How many buttons did the beastly thing have? She struggled with them, wishing that she had a lady's maid whose loyalty she could trust. At last she managed to do up the lower and the upper groups, leaving a great, gaping hole in the middle. It was too late to worry about that. Hurriedly, she brushed her hair and did it up into a loose knot on top of her head.

As all the clocks in the house struck twelve, she threw on her blue velvet cape, picked up her portmanteau, and left her room. Stealing past Cousin Theodora's room, she crept down the stairs and quietly opened the big front door, letting herself out into the night.

11

T HE DARK, DESERTED London street seemed strangely hostile and threatening at midnight. Felicia had been out late before, but always in the company of others. To be alone was very unsettling. She paused cautiously on the front stoop. What if Lord Carlington was late? What would she do then? Perhaps this was a foolish idea after all.

A stab of panic throbbed in her throat as she heard loud, drunken male voices far away, coming from the opposite direction than she was to go. She must take action. She couldn't stay here huddled on the porch of Favoringham House for the pleasure of the young neighborhood bucks. Taking a deep breath, she ran as fast as she could down the sidewalk to the corner and slammed into a large, immovable, *human* form. Felicia screamed, but to her own ears, her cry sounded more like the raspy squawk of a chicken. She looked up and saw, to her relief, Lord Carlington's handsome face.

"Come now, my dear," he said dryly, enfolding her in his arms. "Are you so happy to see me, or is it a bugaboo that you fear?"

Shedding her fear, she stiffly extricated herself

and forgot her resolve to be nice to him. "I am not afraid of anything. And I am not your 'dear'!"

"You are right to be cautious," he went on. "The streets of London are no place for a lady alone at night."

"Well, now I am with you, so it doesn't matter." She glanced uncertainly at the shadowy figures surrounding them. "Who are all these men?"

"My outriders."

"My word! Must you mount an army to take me home?"

"It is wise to be prepared for any eventuality when crossing Hounslow Heath at midnight."

"Are you afraid of highwaymen, my lord?" she baited. "I would never have thought you to be frightened of anything!"

"God help the highwayman who would catch you!"

"Yes, yes. Now tell me, are we to talk the night away, standing where all can see, or are you going to take me to Favoringham Park?"

"Are you sure, Lady Felicia, that you wish to carry through with this?" He looked down at her with a calmness she was far from feeling herself.

"Yes I am." Felicia stepped into the carriage without his assistance. "Please hurry. I shall not feel comfortable until I have left the city."

"I shall not feel comfortable until this whole adventure is finished and behind me." Shannon entered and sat down beside her, rapping his cane on the roof. The coach moved forward.

"I hope those men are close-lipped," Felicia said.

"Of course they are. They're old troopers of mine."

"I might have known." She lowered the hood of her cloak and leaned back against the squabs.

"What is that supposed to mean?"

"Little boys playing at soldiers."

"I'll have you know, Felicia, that there are few jobs available for old soldiers," Shannon pronounced, the edge to his voice telling her that she had finally irritated him. "I do my best to provide employment."

"Bravissimo."

"Damme! Can you never be serious?"

"Yes I can. I would like to know how we arrived on a first name basis, *Shannon*."

"I wasn't aware that we had."

"You called me by my first name."

"I apologize. I didn't realize that I had taken such a grave liberty, but I must admit to being surprised that you even knew what my first name was."

"Hm! I will have you know that I intended to be pleasant to you during this journey. Now I can see that it is impossible. You are entirely too odious."

"And despicable?"

"That, too."

He sighed, resting his head on the cushions. "I'm sorry. It might have been diverting to observe you in a pleasant mood. But what difference does it make? I'm tired anyway. Wake me when we arrive at Favoringham Park."

She did not dignify his comment with a reply. Lord Carlington, as usual, had put her back up. And having done so, he apparently refused to engage in conversation to help the long hours pass.

Felicia closed her eyes and tried to nap, but the swaying carriage caused her gaping dress to rub her back, irritating her skin. "Lord Carlington?"

"Yes," he groaned.

"Would you kindly do up my dress?"

"What?"

"Naturally I couldn't ask my abigail to help me dress for this occasion. Under the circumstances, I think I did rather well." She slipped the cloak from her shoulders. "But I couldn't reach the middle buttons, and it is most uncomfortable."

"Good God!"

"Please? It isn't difficult."

"I know it isn't difficult ..." He paused. "You shouldn't ask me to do it."

Felicia laughed. "You are all I have." She turned her back to him. "Please?" she asked sweetly.

As his hands moved to fasten the row of tiny buttons, the pressure of his fingers caused a warm glow to spread throughout Felicia's body. It was like the feeling she had experienced when she danced with him, but this time it was stronger. Her flesh seemed to burn where his fingers had touched. She swallowed with difficulty, glad when he had finished.

"Thank you, my lord," she whispered, the words nearly sticking in her throat.

"Very well." Shannon's voice was husky. He looked at her for a long moment, then settled himself again, propping up his long legs on the opposite seat.

Pushing aside the strange sensation, Felicia watched the outskirts of London fade from view. They were entering the countryside. The carriage paused while the earl's men extinguished its sidelights.

"Lord Carlington?" She nudged his ribs.

"What is it?"

"Why are the men putting out the lights?"

"This is Hounslow Heath," he said impatiently, "a habitat of ruffians. I would just as soon not have our passage noted."

She leaned forward and peered out the window.

In the absence of moonlight, she could see only a vast darkness. "I don't remember it seeming so very dangerous."

"Most likely, you saw it only in the daylight. Like your street, things seem very different at night, when one is alone."

"But I am not alone. I have you!" Felicia said with forced cheerfulness, refusing to admit how lonely even their large entourage seemed against the blackness of the moor. "And I am not afraid of bugaboos!"

He laughed softly. "The bugaboos out here are real flesh and blood. They'd cut your pretty throat for a shilling."

She shivered, thrusting her arm through his. "Don't frighten me, Shannon. This isn't funny."

"No, it isn't." He covered her hand with his. "First names, Felicia?"

"I didn't realize ... Oh, what does it matter? Anyway, you did it first. Tell me, have you ever seen a highwayman? A Knight of the Road seems very romantic."

"Don't count on it. The highwaymen I've seen, swinging by their necks at Tyburn I might add, were dirty, oafish clods with rotten teeth and no command of the King's English. I don't believe you'd welcome them into your salon."

"Oh, Shannon, have you no sense of adventure?"

"Of course I do. Am I not in the process of kidnapping a duke's daughter?"

"Fiddlesticks!" She laughed. "You cannot kidnap someone who comes willingly. Let us talk of highwaymen again. What would you do if we were waylaid?"

"Attempt to shoot them."

Felicia's eyes widened. "You have a pistol?"

"I and my men are armed to the teeth, madam."

"Oh my! Do you really think there is that much danger in this?"

"I saw no reason to go unprepared."

"I see." Still clinging to his arm, Felicia sank down into the cushions. She hadn't thought that her journey would be hazardous. If it were, she was doubly glad that she had enlisted the aid of the earl. Lord Carlington might be odious at times, but she had no doubt that he could handle even the worst of situations.

"They must be eloping, but this certainly isn't the road to Gretna Green," Tom Garland said in a hushed voice.

"Maybe the lady is ... er ... not a lady, and they're going somewhere else," Sir Everett Halloran murmured.

"If that's the case, Shan'll pay Hell if old Favoringham finds out," Tom said. "Maybe the girl isn't his daughter. Maybe she's just a maid in the house, and Shan's having a little romp with her."

The Earl of Grassham smiled thoughtfully. "It's the duke's daughter all right. If he were going to meet a maid, Shan wouldn't walk right up to the front door like he did this afternoon. Lady Felicia Harding was the girl in the square. I remember her, and you would, too, if you got a good look at her."

"Is she pretty?"

"Very, but she'd be a hell of a handful. Too spirited by half. I'd hate to try to tame her."

"Where could they be going?"

He shrugged. "Who knows? We'll just have to follow along and find out. And let's be quiet about it. I don't want to have to deal with Shan's gang of cutthroats, should they turn on us."

* * *

Shannon stared out at the dismal night. Moonlight might have made travel easier for the horses and coachman, but he was just as glad of its absence. Clandestine deeds should be done in the dark of the moon.

For the hundredth time he wondered why he was doing this. Aiding the flight of a duke's daughter was something that Young Shan, even at his wildest, would never have done. It certainly wasn't proper conduct for the Earl of Carlington. If his family got wind of this, they would disown him, to say nothing of what the ancient members of the House of Lords would think. He would no longer have to worry about discouraging Lady Penelope. Neither she nor her father would ever speak to him again. His career in the government would be finished, his reputation as a gentleman would be besmirched beyond repair, and Lord Favoringham would probably call him out for pistols at dawn. He must have taken leave of his senses to risk everything for this pretty little hoyden.

He shook his head. Well, if all went as planned, at least it would be over soon and he could unload the little baggage at Favoringham Park. With any kind of luck, Lady Felicia Harding would be out of his life forever.

Thank goodness she hadn't accepted his proposal. Shannon still didn't know what had prompted him to make that offer. Marriage to her would have been a complete disaster. He almost laughed, picturing Felicia acting as hostess to his serious new friends in the House of Lords. She could probably turn the most serious political discussion into a total farce. Tom, Ev, and Marcus were the only friends he had who would be entertained by her antics.

His family would have been overcome. His mother would have swooned, and Eliza would have taken to her bed. Edward would have tried to understand, until he met Felicia. Then he would have given up his brother-in-law as a lost cause.

The entire house would have been topsy-turvy. If Felicia directed a household in the same manner as she ran her life, she would hire footmen as maids, and housekeepers as coachmen. There would be breakfast for dinner, beds made up with the spread on the bottom and the sheets on the top, and overall there would be the confusion of no one knowing what they were supposed to be doing.

Grinning at this vision of disaster, Shannon looked down at her. Little Felicia had gone to sleep, her head snuggled against his arm. She was really quite charming in repose, all cute and cuddly and unaware of the social *faux pas* she was committing by lying against him with such familiarity. What a shock this scene would be to the *beau monde*. Compromised again!

But Shannon didn't have the heart to move her. Instead he shifted his numbed arm to encircle her. With an unconscious mew of pleasure, she nestled closer.

Shannon had never held a proper lady this intimately before, and he found that he enjoyed the experience. She smelled so sweet, and her hair was so fine and silky against his cheek. He wondered what it would be like to kiss her.

The coach gave a lurch, and he tightened his embrace to keep her from falling. They drew to an abrupt halt, accompanied by swearing from without. He opened the window.

"Webster?"

"Damn axle's broke, yer lordship."

"The Hell you say!" He sat Felicia up in the seat and removed his arm from her shoulders.

"Shannon . . ." she murmured drowsily.

"I have to get out."

She came fully awake, eyes wide. "What is it?"

"Something's wrong with the carriage."

"Oh dear. Where are we?"

"We're still on Hounslow Heath. You haven't slept long."

"Hounslow Heath!" She reached for him. "Don't leave me!"

"I'll only be outside. There's nothing to be afraid of."

"Shannon!"

He couldn't keep from brushing the loosened hair from her forehead. "It's all right. Don't be frightened."

"I am not." Felicia squared her shoulders. "You have men to take care of things like that. I cannot believe that you would leave me helpless."

"Dammit, Felicia! I'll be just outside the door! If you need me, call."

"There is no need to curse at me."

"I'm sorry." He extricated himself and stepped outside the door.

His minions had lit a lantern and were examining the axle, shaking their heads and swearing under their breath. "It's no use, m'lord. Can't fix that here in the dark. In the morning, we might be able to fix it enough to get us to a decent town, or back to London."

"Damme!" He knelt down to look. "Just my luck!"

"Shannon . . ."

"Females!" he said with exasperation and wondered why his men were grinning. He returned to the door. "What is it?"

"I want to get out and stay with you. I don't like it in here by myself."

"You should have thought of that when you concocted this hare-brained scheme!"

"I didn't know I was to travel with broken-down equipage!"

"This carriage is almost new," he began, then stopped. "Just do as you're told."

"I don't like this a bit."

"Believe me, madam, neither do I!" He strode back toward the front of the disabled coach and overheard the comments from his men.

"Ought to marry her . . ."

"She's a feisty one."

"Be good for 'im!"

The earl cleared his throat, and the whispering ceased. He entered the circle of light. "Well, what are we to do now, gentlemen? Any suggestions? Are any of you familiar with the area?"

One man bashfully stepped forward. "Don't like admitting it, but I am, sir."

"Well?"

"There's an inn a mile or two up ahead, m'lord. Not a place I'd want to take a lady, but with all of us, it should be safe enough. To be sure, we'll need to mount a watch on the horses and on my lady."

He nodded. "That's better than staying here on the road." If he could hide Felicia in a room, they just might be able to escape detection, and he could get her to Favoringham Park without further incident. "Unhitch the horses and we'll start at once."

"Shannon . . ."

Flushing slightly, he returned to the door of the

carriage. This time his old soldiers did nothing to hide their chuckles.

"What are we going to do?" she asked breathlessly.

"There's an inn up ahead. We're going there."

"I can't spend the night with you in an inn!"

"Would you rather spend it here?" he shouted, his temper finally reaching the breaking point.

"No! Oh . . . none of this is happening the way I'd planned it." Her voice trembled. "Please don't yell at me, Shannon."

Gritting his teeth, he willed himself to be calm and soothing with her, despite her provocations. "My dear, I'm doing the best I can. Won't you trust me?"

She nodded solemnly. "Just don't leave me."

"I won't." He lifted her down. "You must do as I tell you, though. No argument."

"No." She slipped into his arms and buried her face in his chest.

Shannon drew her close, gently stroking her back. A burst of desire surged through his veins, nearly taking his breath. He suddenly wished that they would return to their previous antagonism. Felicia Harding, when she exhibited her soft femininity, made him forget that he was standing at night in the middle of Hounslow Heath with a broken-down carriage.

12

FELICIA HELD TIGHTLY to Shannon's arm as they crossed the horrible common room of the inn and started up the steps. She had never been in a place like this before. The outside had been bad enough, even in the dark, with the sagging roof and the filthy, unkempt yard, but the inside was even worse. Cobwebs clung to the dingy, white-washed walls, the floor crunched under her feet, and the dirty, evil-looking men swilling ale called out nasty, embarrassing comments to them as they passed.

"I'm sorry," Shannon had murmured when they had crossed the threshold, "but it seemed the best choice to make. Just stay close to me and don't even look at them."

She had obeyed. Indeed, if she'd gotten any closer to him, he would have had to carry her. For the first time in her life, she experienced real ter-ror. She had been frightened before, at the time when Shannon had caught her in his drawing room, and especially when the axle had broken on the moor, but it was nothing like this. Those men would think nothing, would indeed find amuse-ment, in tearing off her clothes and having their way with her. They could rob and murder Felicia and her escort without batting an eye.

Reaching the top of the stairs, Felicia gasped, realizing that she hadn't taken a breath of air since she had walked through the door. Her heart pounded uncomfortably in her chest, and she couldn't keep her hands from trembling. Light-headed, she leaned even more heavily against the earl.

"Are you all right?" he asked with concern.

She managed to nod.

"Let us see what your room looks like." He fitted a key in a wobbly lock and flung open the creaking door.

Felicia took a step into the chamber, her eyes sweeping over the dusty floor and the drooping bed.

"Not the best of accommodations, but you will be safe. One of us will be outside the door at all times."

"Oh Shannon, don't leave me! You promised!" She flung her arms around his neck. "Please don't leave me!"

He looked at her with shock. "My dear, we've been in some very compromising situations, but this . . ." He shook his head, gently setting her back. "We can't do this, Felicia."

"I'll marry you. I'll do anything! Just please don't leave me here alone!"

"You really are terrified, aren't you?"

"This awful place, those horrible men! Oh, Shannon!"

The tears that had been threatening to come ever since the axle had broken burst forth. Hiding her face in her hands, she sobbed.

"Ssh, ssh . . ." He took her into his arms. "I won't leave you."

"Take care of me!"

"I will, and I'll have you out of here just as soon as I can."

Felicia clung to him. "This is all my fault. I am surprised that you do not go away and leave me here!"

"That would hardly be the gentlemanly thing to do," he said softly, a faint note of teasing entering his voice. He pressed his handkerchief into her hand. "Come now, wipe your eyes and blow your nose."

She obeyed.

"Better now?"

"A little." She lay her head against him, unwilling to break the embrace. It was warm and safe in Shannon's arms. She felt protected.

He lifted her chin. "I need to instruct the men. Why don't you sit down by the hearth? I'll stay right outside the door."

"All right." She allowed him to lead her to a crude, backless bench.

"I won't be long."

He left the door open and stood where Felicia could see him. Even in the candlelight, his handsomeness and commanding presence were unmistakable. She wondered how he had looked in his military uniform. He must have been stunning. And brave. He wouldn't have been mentioned in all those dispatches unless he had exhibited a great deal of courage. Perhaps he deserved his touch of arrogance. She suddenly wished with all her heart that she had not treated him so abominably.

Shannon shut the door behind him and returned to her side. "There! I have posted a guard to scare all the bugaboos away."

Felicia smiled tremulously. "You'll stay with me?"

"Against my better judgment, yes."

"You are so kind to me."

"Did you expect me to be otherwise?"

"No," she said candidly, "but I have been so disagreeable to you in the past, that I should think it would override your scruples. Of course, you made yourself very disagreeable to me, too, but in this instance, it doesn't really signify."

The earl chuckled.

"I fail to find humor in any part of this." She drew herself up. "You are making fun of me."

"It wasn't humor. It was relief that you are returning to normal." He walked over to the fireplace, where a few meager coals glowed. "Somehow I never pictured you to be a clinging vine, even when terrified out of your wits."

She ignored his assessment of her. What did the man want? His precious Penelope Hampstead would certainly be "clinging" in such a situation. Why should he expect Felicia Harding to be any different? Indeed, she wished she could fling herself into his arms, bury her face in his chest, and never look up again until he had removed her from this place. Men were exasperating. One never knew what they wished.

She watched him pull some bark from a log and lay it on the orange embers. "What are you doing?"

"I'm going to try to start up this fire. It's damp and cold in here."

"Can you manage it? Perhaps you should call one of your men."

"Felicia, I did contrive to learn a few things as a soldier. It wasn't one vast, wonderful house party, you know."

"I didn't say it was. I simply wondered at the great Lord Carlington stooping so low as to kindle a fire."

"Don't start that again. Dammit, you can get to me faster than any woman I ever knew!"

"I am uncomfortable. No, it is beyond that. I am miserable."

"That doesn't give you cause to rip it up at me. Besides, as you said, this is all your fault." Shannon bent to blow on the fire. A flame flickered tentatively, then caught, blazing up to bring a cheerful warmth to the dreary bedchamber.

Felicia's spirits rose with the flames. "Well done, m'lord."

He bowed, grinning. "It is more cheerful, isn't it?"

"Yes it is." Shivering, she thrust out her hands to the warmth as he added some of the smaller sticks to the blaze.

A roar of laughter, punctuated with loud talking from below, pierced the oak door.

"How long will that go on?" she asked fearfully.

"What?"

"Those men and their drinking."

"Until they all fall on their faces, I should think."

"It's disgusting!"

"Indeed." Striding across the room he reached into his traveling case and held up a bottle of brandy. "I believe we ourselves could use a drink."

"I've never drunk brandy."

"Now is a good time to experience it."

"We have no glasses."

"No." He popped the cork and took a long swallow from the bottle. "I don't particularly wish to use a glass from this inn, nor to eat anything here either. The landlord's habits of cleanliness are deplorable. The place is probably full of rats, roaches, and bedbugs."

Felicia's eyes widened.

"Have a drink."

She sipped tentatively and coughed. The fiery liquor burnt its way down her throat, but set up a comforting warmth in her stomach. She sipped again.

The earl sat down beside her, drinking deeply. "A little strong for you, isn't it?"

"It is better than nothing, I suppose." She drank again and passed the bottle back to him.

"When this adventure is over, we shall have a glass of good sherry together."

Suddenly dizzy, she leaned against him, giggling. "Have you noticed that this situation really is hilarious? Here we are, Lord Shannon Carlington and Lady Felicia Harding, bonafide members of the aristocracy, sitting on a splintery bench, in a dirty bedchamber, in a vermin-infested inn on Hounslow Heath, drinking brandy straight from the bottle. Oh, what would the *ton* think of this?"

"I can well imagine."

"They would tear our reputations to shreds!" Felicia laughed. "You would lose every scrap of your horrible dignity, Shannon, and I . . . dear me . . ." She shook her head sadly, then brightened. "Just imagine what your precious Lady Penelope would think!"

"She is *not* my precious Lady Penelope."

"It would mean the end of your romance, my lord," she went on, "but never fear. I shall not tell her, even though the temptation is great!"

"I don't care what you tell her. If you think I am

having a romance with Lady Penelope Hampstead, you are sadly mistaken."

She looked at him through a haze. The earl seemed to have two faces. "I . . . I am mistaken?"

"Yes."

"Then I'm very glad." She reached for the bottle, but he held it out of her reach. "I should like to drink to that!"

"I think you've had enough."

"But I'm having a wonderful time, and this indeed is cause for celebration!" Standing, she wobbled to the fireside and sat down on the hearth, removing the pins from her hair and shaking it free. "You and Penelope wouldn't suit. She is a tremendous bore. You would have no one to sharpen your wits upon." She tried to focus on him, but her head spun alarmingly. "I am sorry, my lord. I should like to continue this conversation, but I must . . . I must go to sleep . . ."

Shannon caught Lady Felicia before her hair flew into the fire as she crumpled on the hearth. He carried her to the bed and laid her down, hoping that the inn's vermin indeed did not include lice and bedbugs. What an impossible situation! If it wasn't enough that he be thought guilty of abducting Lord Favoringham's daughter, now he had got her foxed as well. He shook his head. He could never again show his face in the House of Lords. There was only one honorable path to follow. He must go to the duke, confess, beg for Felicia's hand, then retire with her to the country and stay there for the rest of their lives. Sighing, he returned to the fire. He must get some sleep. There would be a lot to face in the morning.

The earl lay down on the floor and tried to doze off. In the bed, Felicia snuggled in with a drowsy murmur and a creaking of ropes. He should have pulled her away from the fire, left her to sleep on the floor, and taken the bed for himself. She'd have never known the difference, but he certainly did. His bones ached, and his muscles cramped.

He got up, went to the bed, and tried to pick her up, but she clung to the edge of the sagging mattress. Swearing lightly, he went around to the other side of the bed, laid his pistol on the side table, and got in. What difference did it make now? He was going to have to marry her anyway. Relatively comfortable, he went to sleep.

Shannon hadn't been asleep long before he was awakened by footsteps in the hall. Listening carefully and hearing no more, he decided it must have been his guards exchanging watches. No longer concerned, he began to extricate himself from the clutches of Felicia who, sometime during his brief nap, had rolled over halfway on top of him, her arm sprawled across his chest and her hair smothering his breath.

"Shannon?"

He turned her onto her back.

"Ooh . . ." She stared up at him, fully sober. "Have I . . . Did you . . ."

He sat up on his elbow. "Nothing happened. Go back to sleep."

The overcast sky had cleared, allowing the moon to shine full force through the grimy chamber window. In its light Felicia's hair seemed to glow with gold dust. Her face, subtly molded by shadow, cheeks tinged prettily, held its own incandescence. Her enormous green eyes softly searched his.

Shannon caught his breath. Felicia Harding might be a hoyden and she might be an exasperating miss, but in this bed tonight, she was very, very much a woman. Too much a woman.

He smiled crookedly. "I'll sleep on the floor."

"Do not discomfort yourself. I trust you." She reached up to touch his cheek. "After all, if nothing has happened thus far, and with me at your mercy . . . I had too much to drink, didn't I?"

"Felicia . . ." His heart raced. Slowly, as if mesmerized by her eyes, he lowered his mouth to hers. Her lips parted gently and her arms encircled his neck, her fingers combing his hair at the nape. "Felicia . . ." He buried his face in her hair, kissing the rapid pulse in her neck.

"Oh, Shannon . . ."

He willed his hand to keep from caressing her where it shouldn't. He had to get up. He couldn't stay here like this, not and retain some small measure of honor.

"I have never been kissed like that," she whispered, dreamily looking up at him. "I wish it to go on and on."

"It can't." With great effort, he pushed himself onto his back.

"Do I disgust you then?" Her voice quivered with tears.

"Good God, no! It's what might happen!"

"I see." It was her turn to raise up on her elbow and look down on him. "You know," she mused, "there is a great deal I do not know about men. About you." She smoothed the hair back from his forehead. "You do not kiss with dignity. You kiss with . . ."

The door crashed open, turning her words into a scream. He flung her to the side and reached for his pistol.

"Wouldn't do that, m'lord! Ain't healthy."

Shannon froze, looking down the barrel of a horse pistol.

"Now that's better, Lord Carlington." The first man was joined by another, as several more hovered in the background. He strode confidently to the table and took the gun, tucking it into his belt. "Must think of your lady, y'know. She's much too pretty to be spoiled by a bloody hole in her forehead."

Shannon leaned back against the head of the bed and drew Felicia to his chest. "What do you want? Money? All we have is on the table. Take it."

"Aw, you're worth more than pocket change, m'lord," the first man said. "We wouldn't have gone to all this trouble for pocket change. No, somebody'll pay dear for you and Lady Carlington."

"I am not . . ." Felicia began.

"Shh." He silenced her. "Where are my men?"

"They're all right, m'lord. At least they will be in a few hours."

"You drugged them."

"Couldn't have taken on all of 'em without you knowing it, now could we?" He grinned.

Shannon clenched his teeth. "Well then, name your price and I'll write a note to my secretary. You'll get your money."

"No note. Can't read it!"

"Then take my lady to him," he said shrewdly. "She'll get your money, but not if you lay a hand on her."

"No!" Felicia cried. "I won't go with them! Please don't make me do that, Shannon! I'm afraid of these people!"

"Dammit, I'm trying to get you away from here," he whispered.

"No lady, and quit that whispering!" The second man inclined his head and spit onto the floor. "You'll come with us."

"Where?"

"A place," he sneered savagely. "Don't be so nosy. Now move!"

The Earl of Grassham stifled a sneeze. The moldy hay in the barn across the road from the disreputable inn was not only irritating his nose, but had made his eyes run as well. He began to wonder if his scheme to spy on Shannon was worth the effort. Here they sat in the dirty, abandoned stable, hungry and thirsty and chilled to the bone.

"Let's go back to London, Marcus," Viscount Garland suggested. "This isn't worth it."

"I'm beginning to agree."

"It's damned uncomfortable here," Ev Halloran put in. "We could have been at White's, playing cards and drinking brandy. Whatever Shan is doing, we'll find out sooner or later."

"It's not long till morning. Shall we wait till first light?"

"Let's go now. The sooner I'm in my bed the better."

They nodded and moved to saddle their horses.

"This was a promising rig, you'll have to admit."

"Just too damn much bad luck."

Marcus Grassham led his horse to the door and opened it, stared, and hastily drew back, closing it to just a slit. "My God! Shan and Lady Felicia are being kidnapped!"

"What?"

"Shh! See if there is a back way out of this place, so we can quickly follow without risk of anyone seeing us from the inn. Did either of you bring a firearm?"

"No. Didn't expect anything like this!"

"Then we'll have to discover where they take them, and ride for help."

The three looked at each other. "We'll not fail," the earl said confidently, "and we'll show Shan what friends are for!"

13

SHANNON'S LAST VIEW, before their captors affixed a blindfold over his eyes, was of Lady Felicia standing fearfully, but with her chin lifted proudly, in the unkempt innyard. Lord, what a travesty this had become. If they got out of it alive, she would never forgive him, nor would she ever let him forget it. She would probably berate him for not facing up to their assailants, but what could he have done? There were too many of them. To attempt to fight them would mean certain suicide, and then what would happen to her? He would have to bide his time and wait for the perfect opportunity to escape, but to manage it with her along might prove to be impossible.

He hoped that their abductors had some shred of honor. Peter Morris, his secretary, would pay whatever they asked, but would it guarantee their freedom? He could recognize them. He would never forget those faces.

He wished that Felicia had taken advantage of the opportunity to escape, when he had suggested that the kidnappers take her to Peter. They would not have dared to touch her with money in the offing. She could have gotten away.

Someone jerked his hands behind him and

wrapped his wrists with rope. "Get on the horse, m'lord."

"You make it rather difficult."

He was unprepared for the blow to his back that sent him stumbling into a horse's shoulder. The animal snorted and skittered away. With difficulty, Shannon regained his balance enough to keep himself from falling to the ground.

"None of yer smart mouth, m'lord!"

"He's right, Rawlings."

"No names, damn you!" There was the resounding smack of a fist hitting flesh and a low moan.

The earl was assisted roughly into the saddle.

"This is not a sidesaddle," Felicia announced scornfully. "It was bad enough that I had to ride astride, earlier. To do so again will surely ruin my dress."

"This ain't no fancy ride in the park, m'lady! And nobody gives a damn about yer dress. Now shut up!"

"I cannot . . ."

"Felicia," Shannon said quietly, "do as they say."

"That's right, little lady. You do as yer man tells you!"

He tensed, hoping that she would follow orders. This was the time that she should return to her previous role of clinging vine. Perhaps without him to lean on, she felt the need to assert herself. Couldn't she realize that men like this would have no patience with her? The one who had hit him was in no mood to bandy words. It would make no difference to him whether he struck a man or a woman.

With relief he heard her sniff deprecatingly, then fall silent. He shook his head. Even if it was only a gesture, Felicia Harding had had the last say.

The horses started out at a walk. Shannon tried

to ascertain their direction and decided that they were continuing east on the main road. But when they struck a trot he was too busy at first with adjusting his balance to notice. After what seemed like an hour at the very least, they slowed to a walk and turned abruptly. He caught the scent of wet, moldering leaves and felt a damp mist on his face. By the muffled sounds of the horses' hooves, they must be entering a woodland. Another horse came alongside his.

"Shannon, is that you?" Felicia whispered.

"Yes."

"What are we going to do?"

"Wait."

"My legs are aching so." Her voice rose. "This awful . . ."

"No talkin'!" an angry voice ordered.

"Obey them and wait," he murmured, and immediately felt a pistol muzzle poke into his back.

"I see no harm in speaking quietly . . ." Felicia began.

"Shut up, woman! M'lord, is your lady always this much trouble?"

"Much more so," Shannon said grimly.

There were several light guffaws. "You should smack her mouth bloody!"

"That is a disgusting thing to say!" Felicia cried angrily.

A rough hand grasped Shannon's collar and jerked him backwards. "You either shut that woman up, m'lord, or I'll do it for you! I'm tired to death with the both of you."

"Felicia," he ordered sternly, "for God's sake, do as they say."

"But . . ."

"Felicia!"

She repeated her expressive sniff and fell silent.

They rode on for a short time and gradually the scent of decaying vegetation lifted and the air freshened. Shannon sensed that they were in a meadow, and a low one at that, from the squishing of their footsteps. At last they drew to a halt.

One of their captors jerked him off his horse and prodded him forward. "Welcome to your new home, m'lord."

His boots struck stone. They must be entering a building with flagged floors. A heavy odor of damp mustiness assailed his nostrils.

"Get ready to go down some steps. Now."

He started down, hearing Felicia's light feet trip and her insolent, "Don't touch me, you filthy brute!" Dear Lord, if only she would keep her mouth shut! Where was her speechless terror of before? Shannon reached the foot of the steps and paused.

"You'll stay here. No point in shouting for help for none will hear ye! When we get the money, we'll set ye free."

"It's freezing in here, and damp," Felicia complained. "How can you leave us in a place like this? We'll catch our death. I am cold, and I'm hungry."

"Shut up!"

"The least you could do is . . ."

"Felicia . . ." Shannon began, when something heavy struck the back of his head. Lights danced, and he felt himself falling.

"You didn't have to do that!" Felicia, her blindfold removed, cried.

"You want the same thing, m'lady?" The man who was untying her hands gave her a painful jerk. "If you'd have kept yer mouth shut, none of that would have happened!"

"You may have killed him!"

"Naw. His Lordship'll just have a nice little sleep and a bit of a headache later."

"You despicable people!"

He laughed and moved to the unconscious Earl of Carlington, stripping the signet ring from his finger. "My proof," he said to her. "We'll be rich."

"I hope you never see a shilling of it!" she hissed. "I hope you're caught and strung up by the neck!"

"You'd better not hope for them things, m'lady. If that'd happen, you and yer fine lord'll be nothing but meat for the rats!" He spit at her. "Now don't you go trying to escape. I'm leaving men to watch you, men who'd sooner cut yer throat as look at yer!"

One of his cronies entered, carrying a bucket of water.

"This'll tide you over. Enjoy yer stay, Countess. Spend yer time nursing yer fine lord back to health instead of working yer mouth." He withdrew, drawing shut a heavy oak door behind him.

Felicia heard a lock snap into place. "Shannon!" she screamed, running to his sprawled body. "Oh, my dear Shannon!"

She knelt beside him, shuddering at the jagged cut on the back of his head, the blood flowing freely. Why had they done that to him? There had been no need!

She felt for his pulse and could have cried with happiness at its strength and steadiness. Hastily she ripped off her petticoat and began to tear it up. Making a thick pad, she sat down on the floor, his head cushioned in her lap, and began to staunch the flow of blood.

"Oh Shannon, I'm so sorry," she sobbed. "This is all my fault! If I'd not spoken out . . . Oh, if I'd only put up with Cousin Theodora and forgotten my pride, or if I had agreed to marry you, none of this would have happened! Now you will truly hate me!"

She thought of how he had kissed her in the night and cried harder. He wasn't the way she had thought he was on the morning she stood in the square before Carlington House. Beneath his cool public exterior, he was warm and affectionate. He had showed her that, but she would never see it again.

They would be discovered. After all the compromises of yesterday and today, the Earl of Carlington would feel honor-bound to marry her. But he wouldn't want to, and she would refuse him, even though her father would insist upon it now. She would simply disappear from Society and live quietly until her death on one of her father's or brother's estates.

Lord Shannon Carlington would go on to be a master statesman. He would marry a proper lady, who would support him in achieving his goal. His wife would never step a foot out of line or have a curl out of order. She would give him beautiful, well-mannered children. They would be very happy.

Felicia's throat constricted painfully. "But I don't *want* anyone else to kiss you!" she wept. "I want to be all those things to you. If only I could do it all over again!"

But even if she could erase everything that had happened, it wouldn't serve her purpose. If she hadn't been naughty, she would never have met him. He had been looking for a proper lady, and he hadn't paid the slightest heed to her. He wanted someone like Lady Penelope Hampstead.

She closed her eyes. She seemed to remember

something, in a blur, that he had told her when they were drinking the brandy together. It was about Penelope. Had he said that he didn't care for her?

Felicia's heart pounded. Maybe that was it! Perhaps he had come to care for her instead of Penelope! How could he have kissed her the way he had, if he had no feeling for her? If only he cared for her still, she would never again give him cause for irritation. She would do exactly as he said, and she would be the most proper lady in London. She would show them all.

She started, as a key rasped in the lock. The door opened to reveal a tall, husky youth holding a blanket. He grinned foolishly and stared at her with blank, bovine eyes.

"Pretty lady want blanket?"

She eyed him warily.

"Pretty lady want blanket?" he repeated, stepping forward. "I like pretty lady."

Her muscles tensed. He was a half-wit. There was a girl of similar affliction on her father's estate. Childlike, but possessing the body of an adult, she belonged in no one's world. She was easily influenced and was often taken advantage of by boys reaching their maturity. Felicia had felt sorry for her and had seen that she received work under the protective wing of Mrs. Jacobs, Favoringham's fearsome housekeeper. After that, no one had dared lay a hand on little Goldie.

But this was different. The youth before her was a young man. And she and Shannon were at his mercy. She lay her arm protectively across the earl's chest. "I would like to have the blanket," she said quietly, "but you cannot come any farther. My lord must not be disturbed."

"He hurt."

"Yes he is, but he will be better soon."

"I like pretty lady."

"Then you. must do as I say."

"I help. Nobody know."

"Nobody knows?"

He shook his head. "Lady cold, so I come."

Felicia wished with all her heart that Shannon had not been unconscious. Together they might have made an escape, but she would be frightened to try it alone. Furthermore, she couldn't possibly leave him.

"I am glad you have brought me a blanket. Please leave me now and go. Someone will miss you and come looking. They might be angry."

"I help." He came forward and flung the blanket around Felicia's shoulders. "Pretty lady be warm now." He stroked her hair.

Felicia could scarcely control her cringe. "You must go," she said firmly. "You know you are not supposed to be here. Someone will . . ."

"Billy!" The door banged backwards on its hinges. "You damned fool . . ."

The youth took to his heels, running past the swarthy, heavyset man and up the narrow stone stairway.

"I tell you, woman, if we catch you causing trouble one more time . . .!"

"I certainly had nothing to do with this!" she snapped.

"You've bewitched the poor fool!"

"I most certainly have not! I never laid eyes on him until this moment!"

"You shut up, or I'll give your lord a good kick in the jaw!"

Felicia flung herself over Shannon. "You must kick me first!"

Holding her breath, she waited for the hobnailed boot to strike her, but the door slammed shut, and she heard heavy stomping on the steps. Cautiously she sat up and looked around. He had gone and, thank God, he had left her the blanket. Sweeping it off her shoulders, she covered Shannon and waited fearfully for their next visitor.

Marcus Grassham, Thomas Garland, and Everett Halloran drew back into hiding and stared at each other as the party of men passed.

"My count tells me that they've left three of them on guard," Marcus stated.

The others agreed.

"They're armed, I'm sure, but do you think we could take them?" Tom ventured.

"If it were only Shan ..." The earl shook his head. "It's just too risky, especially with the lady present. And we don't know the plan of the place, or where they've placed them. Damme! If we only had weapons!"

"Well, who would have thought? We didn't even know we were leaving town." Ev shrugged. "What next, Marcus? You seem to be our captain."

"We'll have to go for help. Back to London, I think. Those brigands will plan to extract ransom, unless I miss my guess, so we've got a bit of time on our side. I wouldn't be surprised if they didn't stop at that inn on the way to tip a few in celebration. That should give us time."

"I'll stay here," Ev said, "to make sure that nothing new develops. If those ruffians happen to move them, I'll follow. So if I'm not here when you return with reinforcements, wait. Somehow I'll get word to you."

Marcus nodded. "Once Tom and I get to London, one of us will go to Shan's secretary and tell him to stall. The other will go to Torrence, his brother-in-law."

"What about Favoringham?"

The three winced.

"We'll let Torrence handle that," Marcus said flatly. "Rescuing them is our concern. The Favoringham situation is a family matter."

They agreed. "This is all our fault, you know," Ev said slowly. "If we hadn't come up with that hare-brained scheme about the women, none of this would have happened. Whatever is going on, we're the ones who placed the Lady Felicia and Shan together."

"Well, I don't know if I agree with that." The earl frowned. "But at least we're trying to do something about it. Let's be on our way."

The two nodded their good-byes to their friend and led their horses through the brush. Once out of sight of the ancient, derelict abbey, they mounted and walked on cautiously.

"Once we're on the highway, we can pass them if we wish. We'll just be ordinary travelers."

Reaching the road, they broke their mounts into a canter. They didn't gain sight of the kidnappers until they passed the shabby inn. There, several horses were tied outside.

"Just like I thought," Marcus said. "I wonder what happened to Shan's men."

Tom winced, not liking to be reminded that other lives were involved as well.

They put a half-mile's distance between them and the inn and brought their horses down to a walk to give them a breather.

"It is our fault, Marcus. If we hadn't meddled . . ."

"I don't even want to think about it!" the earl snapped.

"We were just too damn proud to admit that Shannon didn't want to be our friend anymore. And maybe he's right in that. We're too old for the foolishness we engage in."

"Believe me, Tom, this is the last. For me, at least!"

"You're serious?"

"I don't know what's going on, or whether we caused it, but I'm going to take my seat in the House, and I'm going to see to my estates, instead of paying someone else do it. I think I'll even go to Almack's and find myself a wife."

Tom stared at him. "My God, you are serious!"

"Our pranks *are* getting a little ridiculous. You're right. We're too old for them."

"Well, then, I just might join you in the endeavor." He grinned. "Of course I can't take up my seat until Papa cocks up his toes, but he did give me a nice estate in Hampshire."

"Wait until you see me approach the Duke of Torrence," Marcus said smugly. "You will witness proper decorum and perfect dignity."

"Bravo!"

"But when I approach the kidnappers, you will see the skill of Gentleman Jackson's salon and, perhaps, the crudity of the gamekeeper of Grassham Hall!"

Tom raised an eyebrow. "From me, you will see the hidden horrors of Harrow."

"Then on to the rescue!" Marcus kicked his horse into full gallop and sped down the London road.

14

IT WAS MID-MORNING before Marcus Grassham leaped off his weary horse, tied him to the hitching post, and ran up the steps two at a time to pound on Lord Torrence's door. It was a shock to the duke's staid butler, who had never before seen a visitor in such disarray. When the young earl would have pushed past him, the butler, remembering the attack on Lord Carlington's house, valiantly blocked the way.

"I must speak with Lord Torrence just as quickly as possible!" Marcus cried, forgetting his vow of dignity and trying to dart past the august personage. "It's a matter of life or death!"

Fielding held to the door jamb. "His Grace is at breakfast. No one disturbs . . ."

"He'll see me! Shan's in trouble! Lord Carlington, that is. Don't stand there gawking, man! Let me in!"

"Your name, sir?"

"Grassham."

"Wait here, my lord." Fielding allowed the visitor entry to the hall. "I shall inform His Grace."

"Oh, botheration!" Marcus ran past him through the house, opening doors as he went along.

"My lord!" cried the frantic butler.

153

"Torrence! Where are you!"

"Stop that, my lord! This is highly irregular!"

The earl flung open the breakfast-room door to reveal His Grace, half rising from his chair, and his white-faced lady.

"Marcus!" Lady Torrence cried, relieved to see that this was not a berserk madman. "Whatever are you doing, frightening us like this?"

"Good God, Eliza, don't go into a decline!" Marcus shut the door in the butler's face and leaned against it. "We haven't time for that. Shan's in trouble! He and Felicia Harding have been kidnapped!"

"Felicia Harding!" Shannon's sister groped for her smelling salts. "Edward . . ."

Her husband retrieved her vinaigrette and waved it under her nose.

"I don't know what is going on between them," Marcus said apologetically, suddenly realizing the shock he had given them.

His wife restored to benumbed consciousness, the duke turned to Grassham. "Sit down, Marcus, and catch hold of yourself. Then tell us what has happened."

The earl took a deep breath and sat down. "Last midnight, Shan picked up the Lady Felicia Harding on a corner near her house."

"Eloping!" Eliza said with horror. "With Felicia Harding! Edward, that is Favoringham's daughter. Mama will have a conniption!"

"Let Marcus continue, dear."

"As part of a prank," the earl explained, the blood suffusing his cheeks, "we, er . . . Ev, Tom, and I, followed them. They proceeded across Hounslow Heath until the carriage broke an axle. Then they rode on to an inn." He cleared his throat. "Not a very nice establishment, Your Grace, but I suppose they had no choice ... if they were avoiding returning to London."

Eliza closed her eyes and dramatically leaned back her head. "How could he! What will Lady Penelope think? To say nothing of her father!"

"Yes, yes." Lord Torrence began to pace the floor. "Please go on."

"We hid in a barn, but grew cold and weary of it, and decided to leave. That's when we saw Shan and Lady Felicia, tied and blindfolded, being abducted by a group of men. Shan had had a number of his men with him, too. I don't know what happened to them.

"So we followed. They took them to what looks to be the ruins of an old priory. Ev stayed there, hidden in the woods, to watch the place while Tom and I came for help. We assumed the kidnappers would ask for ransom, so Tom went to warn Shan's secretary to wait for your decision," he finished lamely.

The duke halted. "You did the right thing."

"Thank you, sir."

"Oh, what are we to do?" Eliza wailed. "When people hear of Shannon and Felicia Harding ..."

"Right now, my dear, Shannon's and the lady's safety is more important than what people will think of this. We'll gather some men and attempt the rescue. Grassham, do what you can on that score." He strode into the hall, with his wife and the earl trailing him. "I'll meet you at Carlington House. I ... I suppose I must go to Lord Favoringham first."

Eliza wrung her hands. "What will you say to him, Edward? He will want Shannon to marry his daughter! You must extract my brother from this situation."

"That, my dear, is not my business. I am going

only to inform Lord Favoringham of his daughter's whereabouts, and to hope for his assistance."

His wife stamped her foot. "He can't marry her! Mama won't approve!"

Footsteps from above caught Eliza's attention. Fearfully glancing upward, she cringed against her husband.

"What is all this uproar!" Lady Carlington demanded from the balcony. "All this running and shouting has sorely disturbed my rest. Torrence, I insist upon an explanation!"

"Go to your mother." The duke gave his wife a gentle push.

"But you are so much better with her than I am!" she pleaded.

"I am going to help your brother." He gave her a brief kiss on the forehead. "Go now."

"Torrence! Eliza!"

"I am coming, Mother." She started slowly up the stairs, feet dragging, as she watched her husband and the earl rush out, leaving her to deal with her mother.

"Hurry, gel!"

"Mama, I am quite overset. I am coming just as fast as I can."

"Fustian! Nine times out of ten when you say you are overset, it is a falsity designed to excite the sympathy of that besotted husband of yours. Don't try to fob off your delicate condition on me! When I carried you and Shannon, I never felt better in my life!"

Eliza reached the top of the steps. "Let us go into the little sitting room." She glanced at her mother's maid hovering in the background. "Jeannette, please bring us tea."

"I always have chocolate in the morning," Lady Carlington snapped.

Her daughter nodded. "See to it, Jeannette." She ushered her mother into the small parlor. "You had best sit down, Mama. You aren't going to like this."

"So I have gathered."

"It's about Shannon."

"Oh, what has he done this time!"

"He has run off with a lady, and they have been kidnapped."

"Run off with a lady!" her mother cried. "Not Penelope Hampstead? No, there would be no reason to run off with her. Lord Baywater likes him . . ."

"It's Lady Felicia Harding."

"Felicia Harding! Favoringham's wild daughter?"

"She is very pretty," Eliza ventured nervously, "and truly she is simply high-spirited, not really wild."

"She's a fast little flirt!"

"That may be, Mama, since you are always right. But at this moment, shouldn't we be more concerned for their safety, rather than about any scandal which may result?"

"It is a dilemma that must be faced," Lady Carlington said firmly.

"But surely not now? Perhaps there is a perfectly good explanation for everything."

"I doubt it! Your brother has reverted to his old ways. This is exactly the kind of thing he would have done in the past, and exactly the type of chit who would have attracted him! All is lost."

Eliza regarded her helplessly. "Let us rely on Shannon's good sense."

"He has none! I shall never speak to him again!" she vowed. "Running off with Felicia Harding! What about poor Lady Penelope? However shall I

face her family again?" Putting her hands to her
forehead, Lady Carlington swooned onto the sofa.

Shannon opened his eyes to a splitting headache. Looking uncomprehendingly at the damp,
gray stone wall, he gradually remembered the ab-
duction up to the point when he had been struck
in the back of the head. Where was he now? And
where was Felicia? He struggled to sit up.

"Shannon!" she cried joyously. "You are awake!"

"Felicia?" He allowed her to push him gently
back down onto her lap, inhaling her faint scent of
eau de cologne.

"Oh my darling, I have been so worried! You
were unconscious for so very long!"

Darling? A cool, wet cloth smoothed his throbbing forehead. He closed his eyes, giving himself
up to her sweet ministrations. "My head is bursting."

"I know it must be. You have a very bad cut, but
I managed to stop the bleeding. Head wounds
bleed so much! I know, for once I fell from an apple tree and cut my head. It took Nurse the longest
time to patch me up."

Only Felicia could talk of falling from an apple
tree in a situation such as this, when other young
ladies would be fainting with fear. Somehow it
was soothing. If he hadn't been so worried about
her safety, he would be glad that she was here
with him.

"Did you ever climb a tree again?" he asked
inanely.

"Oh yes," she sighed, "and I fell again. I never
learn my lessons well. If I did, I don't suppose that
we would be here in this situation. I'm so very
sorry. Can you ever forgive me?"

"If you can forgive me for meddling in your affairs."

"Most easily." She laughed lightly. "I would never have known you if you hadn't, and I very much enjoy knowing you, my lord."

He enjoyed knowing her, too, more than he could say, even though she was the most exasperating woman he had ever met. He enjoyed her lightning changes of mood, her quick wit, and her minx-like beauty. He'd enjoyed the kiss they had shared and had been tantalized by its fiery promise. Felicia was a creature of challenge, and no man would ever really be her master. She would only let him think he was. For some unexplainable reason, it seemed appealing.

Shannon cleared the thoughts of her from his head. There would be time later to consider his feelings for her. He must think of a way out of their current dilemma.

His secretary, Peter Morris, would pay the ransom. There was no question about that. But would they be released? It would cause a great deal of risk to their captors. Peter would likely have them followed and make an attempt at capture. If that failed, there was still the fact that he and Felicia might recognize them. It would be much easier for the abductors to take the money and never return, leaving them to die in this prison. Or to kill them. There was no question about it. He and Felicia must try to escape.

He sat up. "What kind of place is this? An old dungeon?"

"More like a cellar. There are passages. Shannon, I don't believe you should sit up just yet. Your head . . ."

"We have to get out of here if we can. I'll think about my head later."

He looked around the large stone room. Illuminated by two high and tiny windows, it was bare of any contents, other than an old, rotten barrel. The ceiling was hung with moldering spider webs. On one wall was a heavy oak door, through which they must have come, and on two others were arched openings to passageways.

"Shannon, I think we should stay where we are. These are horrible men. If they caught us trying to escape, they might do us terrible damage." She told him of her experience with the youth, and the discovery by the other man. "He would take pleasure in finding an excuse to beat us."

"I don't trust any of them. They might take their money and leave us here . . . or kill us. Come, Felicia." He stood, caught her hand, and drew her to her feet. "We'll explore the passages."

The sudden movement made him dizzy. His head throbbed even more painfully, and his stomach threatened to disgorge its meager contents. He swayed slightly.

"Shannon, you cannot do this!" Felicia caught his waist. "You are ill! Please be reasonable!"

"I am." He leaned on her slightly, as his head cleared. "You've said yourself that the men are dangerous. Do you think they care what happens to us?"

"No . . ."

"Then come." He took her hand and started toward the nearest passageway. "Trust me."

Felicia planted her feet and refused to budge. "I trusted you before, and see where it landed me. From the first moment you decided to transport me across Hounslow Heath in an unreliable carriage, I should have known that I could not depend on you!"

"*I* decided!" He whirled around to face her. "I

seem to recall your begging me to take you to your home, the direction of which happens to lie across Hounslow!"

"I *asked*. I didn't beg. And I certainly did not expect to ride in a carriage that was ready for the woodpile!"

"I bought that carriage new, last winter!"

"Then the maker must have seen you coming," she said smugly.

"Dammit, Felicia! Why must you argue with me all the time?"

"Because you often make the wrong decisions. You make decisions concerning me without consulting me!"

"Very well," he said shortly. "You stand there and make your own decisions. I'm going to explore this passage."

A sense of panic stabbed her stomach as Felicia watched Shannon's angry strides carry him through the archway and into the semi-darkness beyond. She was sure he would come for her if he found a way of escape. He was too honorable a man not to do that. But what if the kidnappers returned before he came back? What would they do to her? Shannon had no weapon, but she felt much safer with him than she did alone, and there was more to it than that. He had suffered a hard blow to the head. What if he became dizzy and fainted? What if she couldn't find him? What if the kidnappers returned for her and left him there to die?

"Shannon!" she cried, springing after him. "Shannon, wait!"

He paused and turned just inside the arch.

"I'm sorry!" She flung herself onto his chest, glad when his arms wrapped around her. "You are

right, of course! I don't know why I argue with
you. I shall never do so again!"

He chuckled lightly. "Never is a long time, Felicia."

"I shall contrive!"

"I don't know that I want to spend the rest of
my life without your defiance. It sounds rather
boring."

Tears gathered in her eyes. "If we escape this episode, you shall never see me again."

"On the contrary, my dear, I shall probably see
you every day. We shall be married, you know."

"No." She shook her head. "I won't force you to
that. Nor shall I permit my father to do so."

He lifted her chin and Felicia looked into his
wonderful eyes. Slowly his lips came down on
hers, gently, but with a hint of the passion of the
previous night. She clung to him as her knees
turned to water.

The kiss deepened. As he drew her closer, she
could feel the hard lines of his body pressing
against her softness. It was frightening, but exhil-
arating, and it seemed just right. He wanted her.
With shock, she realized that she wanted him, too.

It had to stop. There were other things they
must think of now. Later, when they were free of
this prison, she could sort out her unfamiliar feelings and thoughts.

She touched his cheek and turned her head. "We
mustn't do this."

"No," he murmured in a husky and slightly be-
wildered voice. He hugged her close for a moment
and let her go. "When this is over . . ." The words
trailed away. "Let us continue our search."

"Very well." Felicia slipped her hand in his, her
nerves soothed by his touch.

The passageway was damp and colder than the

room they had been in. On its sides, doors opened, sagging on worn hinges, to reveal dark, empty rooms. Touching the wall, Felicia found it moist.

"Can we be near water, Shannon? A river, perhaps? Everything here is so wet."

"I think we are. Did you notice the horses' hooves squishing in the ground? It reminded me of a water meadow. I hope I'm right."

"Why?"

"If this place is near a river, there might be a tunnel to it, built so people could easily transport supplies to and from boats."

"Oh. But why go to all the trouble of digging a tunnel for that?"

The corridor came to a dead end and turned abruptly. Peering into a dark room, Shannon drew her inside. "Look. I was right!"

Felicia glanced around at the crumbling wooden racks lining the walls. "It's a wine cellar."

"Exactly. I think many of these rooms were wine cellars. I'll wager we're in the wine-making area of an old priory or monastery. And what easier way to transport their wine to market than by a tunnel leading to the river, where it was then placed on boats?" He clutched her shoulders. "Maybe we'll be in luck!"

She smiled doubtfully. "But why would those men have put us in a place where we could just walk out? Surely they would be familiar with it."

"Maybe it's caved in. We might have to dig out."

"With what?"

"Don't be such a pessimist, Felicia. Come, let's go further!"

"What if they catch us?"

He made a snort of disgust. "Do you want out of here or not?"

"Yes, but . . ."

"You promised not to argue with me."

"Well, yes, I did, but . . ."

"No 'buts'!" He took her hand again and vigorously pulled her out of the room and down the passageway.

15

Tʜᴇ Dᴜᴋᴇ ᴏꜰ Torrence dreaded his mission to Favoringham House and wished he could have done anything but confront the old lord, of whom he had only slight acquaintance. Favoringham would have discovered his daughter's absence by now and would be in no mood for civilities, especially when he learned what Edward had to tell him. He would probably cut up quite dreadfully, and maybe even call out Shannon for pistols at dawn.

Painfully, the duke had to admit to himself that his brother-in-law deserved it. He had sympathized with him over the Penelope Hampstead affair, but this act was beyond all reason. If he had wanted the little chit, why couldn't he have gone about it in an honorable way? It was just like the Shannon of old to do something stupid like this.

Edward was bitterly disappointed. His brother-in-law had exhibited such promise. He'd shown responsibility, sophistication, and intelligence. And now this! Didn't he give a fig about how the affair affected the rest of the family? When he saw him again, and hopefully he would, Edward intended to tell Shannon exactly what he thought.

Getting off his horse, he strode up the steps to

Favoringham House and let fall the heavy brass knocker. He took a deep breath. The situation was going to require every bit of tact and taste he could muster.

"Good day, sir."

Edward nodded to the butler and presented his card. "I am the Duke of Torrence. I have come to see Lord Favoringham on a matter of the utmost urgency."

"One moment, sir."

Cooling his heels in the entry, the duke reflected upon what he remembered of Lord Favoringham and his daughter. The man was said to be very wealthy and, like him, was a member of the House of Lords. In politics, he was a Whig. Known for his sense of humor, he was a popular figure at the various gentlemen's clubs. Torrence wished Lord Favoringham might retain his joviality in the interview to come, but he knew that was too much to ask for.

He couldn't recall ever meeting Lady Felicia, but Eliza seemed to consider her objectionable. The girl's family background was impeccable. It must be something about her address or manner that set up his wife's back.

"Sir? If you will come this way?"

Edward followed the stiff-backed servant up the stairs and into a charming sitting room. Within sat the very sober duke and a drab, red-eyed, elderly lady. He bowed.

Lord Favoringham stood, returning the courtesy. "Torrence, may I introduce you to my cousin, Miss Theodora Pixley?"

"Ma'am." He leaned politely over her limp hand.

"My butler told me you had come on a matter of some urgency. I dislike asking you to come to the point at once, sir, but we have had something of an upset in the house."

Torrence clenched his jaw. "I fear that my urgent matter has something to do with that upset, Your Grace."

"Felicia!" cried the cousin, bursting into tears. "Something has happened to her!"

Lord Favoringham started, narrowing his eyes. "You know something about my daughter?"

"Yes, I do." He flicked his eyes toward the weeping lady. "Perhaps we should discuss it alone."

"My Felicia! My dear, sweet Felicia!" the lady sobbed. "What horrible thing has befallen her? Do not spare me! I must hear it, too!"

"If you stay to hear this, Cousin Theodora," Favoringham said anxiously, "you will cut this weeping and keep a still tongue in your head! Go on, Torrence. Ignore the woman."

Edward had no wish to repeat the delicate tale in front of a nearly hysterical lady, but he had no choice, and time was wasting. He plunged ahead. "Your daughter is in the company of my brother-in-law, Lord Carlington, and the two of them have been kidnapped."

"Oh!" Cousin Theodora shrilled.

"Be still, woman!" Lord Favoringham shouted. "Now tell me what you know of this. I have received no ransom demands!"

Torrence repeated what the Earl of Grassham had told him, adding, "We are gathering as many men as possible to ride after them."

"Count me in." He stalked to the bellpull and rang it impatiently. "Just wait till I get hold of that gel!"

The butler, who must have been standing just outside with his ear pressed to the door, entered.

"Murray, quickly mount a force of as many of my servants who wish to go on an armed mission of rescue. Lady Felicia has been abducted!" He turned to Torrence. "I'll have plenty of volunteers. Anything out of the ordinary is a high treat for my staff."

"She said she was going to Favoringham Park. She said nothing about *him!*" Cousin Theodora bleated. "He must marry her, of course. Lord have mercy on us all! I knew he was a cad."

"Favoringham Park?" Edward asked.

"A note from my daughter." Lord Favoringham waved a scrap of paper in his face. "She wrote that she was going home to the country. She fled sometime during the night."

"I should have locked the ungrateful girl in her room," the cousin said angrily, her tears miraculously ceasing.

"Then they weren't eloping?"

"How do I know? The girl is full of tricks!" she spat.

"My daughter," sighed Lord Favoringham, "has been known to cast red herrings. Well, no matter. Your brother will certainly marry Felicia when this is done with."

"Brother-in-law," Torrence corrected, unwilling to admit blood relationship with the black sheep. "I'm sure Shannon will do what is honorable."

"You will see to it?" Cousin Theodora screeched.

"That won't be necessary, ma'am. I assure you Lord Carlington is a man of honor." He glanced pointedly at Felicia's father. "Time is of the essence, sir."

"Indeed. Where shall I meet you?"

"I'll be at Carlington House."

"Very well. I'll join you there immediately."

"I shall accompany you," the lady announced.

"Oh, no, you will not!"

Torrence let himself out the door.

"I cannot sit here waiting, with nothing to do!"

"That's exactly what you will do! If you had handled Felicia gently, like one would treat a high-strung filly, she would not have run away from home!"

"She is not a horse! She is a naughty little girl who wants discipline!"

Torrence hurried down the stairs, their voices following him. He wondered what on earth Shannon had been thinking of when he had gotten himself involved in this escapade. But that didn't matter now. He had become involved with the Favoringham family, and it seemed likely that he would remain so.

Cutting through alleys, he arrived at the back of Carlington House, where a small army was assembling. His own servants, and those of Grassham and his friends, had been joined by Shannon's men, who had their own story to tell of drugged ale and a subsequent awakening to find the empty chamber. They had cracked some skulls before they left the inn, but had received no further information. So they did the only thing they could. With their horses stolen, they returned on foot to London, in hopes that their master might have already been ransomed and released, and that he would be understanding enough to forgive them.

The duke's head began to ache when he heard that Shannon and Felicia had shared a bedroom. Was there no end to the indiscretions? None of their families would be able to lift their heads in Society after this news was spread. He swore the little army to secrecy, but he had no hope that the scandal would remain unknown to London. Damn his brother-in-law! If he weren't so worried for

Shannon's safety, he'd let him stew in his own juice!

He went inside and found Peter Morris calmly discussing the situation with the Earl of Grassham.

"Has anyone come for ransom yet?"

"No, Your Grace, and if they see this crowd, I doubt they will. Furthermore, they'll become suspicious."

"Damme! I didn't think of that! Let's hope they approach by the alley. Let's go, Grassham. We'll meet up with Favoringham on the way."

"Your Grace?" Mr. Morris asked. "When, and if, they come, shall I give them the money?"

"Within reason. If the demands are excessive, stall for time." He started for the door.

"Sir?"

Torrence paused.

"What is reasonable, sir? What is Lord Carlington worth?"

"At present, not a shilling!" Edward snarled and hurried out.

Joined by the forces of the Duke of Favoringham, the army of servants clattered out of London. Favoringham's troops were not as impressive as the ex-soldiers of Torrence and Carlington Houses, but what they lacked in experience, they made up for in spirit. At their head was the old duke himself, accompanied by the young marquess, who wore a dangerously revengeful expression on his face. They had brought a closed carriage to discreetly convey the unfortunate lady home.

Despite a certain concern for Lord Carlington and Lady Felicia, the men enjoyed the holiday atmosphere. No one, when he had gotten up that morning, had expected to be armed and mounted on a fine horse, setting off on an adventure. Besides, this wouldn't be the only day of amusement. After what had happened, there was sure to be a wedding to come.

Lord Torrence's servants were the quietest ones. They knew that the duke and duchess, and that high stickler, Lady Carlington, were very displeased. They had no wish to court the temper of His Grace, but they listened to the others, threw in a comment now and then, and hid their excitement.

The Duke of Favoringham's troops sided with their Lady Felicia. Whatever sin she had committed, she had been driven to it by that nasty Cousin Theodora. They hoped that old Favoringham would realize that and treat the sweet young lady with kindness. Most of all, they hoped that Lord Carlington would be a loving husband to her. She deserved better than she had been getting in the past few weeks.

Shannon's men felt the thrill of potential battle. "Just like old times, ain't it? And we've got two dukes and an earl at our head!"

"We can't fail!"

"We won't! Never! We'll bring 'em home all right and tight!"

"We'll get our revenge!"

"And a new countess!"

The old soldiers guffawed. "Won't she lead him a merry dance?"

With images of the young lady trimming the earl into shape, they marched on to war.

The entrance to the tunnel was marked by a heavy, pithy oak door, which had fallen off its hinges and been propped up against the wall. Inside, the passage narrowed and its ceiling lowered. Built of brick, it showed signs of crumbling.

"Look at this!" Shannon pawed at a niche in the wall. "Candles! And tinder!"

"That means that someone uses this tunnel," Felicia said ominously.

"Not necessarily. These things could have been here for a long time."

"They haven't, Shannon. I know they haven't. Those men are smart. They know about this tunnel, and they wouldn't have left us here if they knew we could escape through it. They'll catch us, and they'll beat us. They might even kill us! Please, let us go back!"

"Not now." He struck fire to one of the tapers. "I'm going to see where this leads."

Felicia angrily stamped her foot. "You are acting just like a little boy on some sort of make-believe adventure. I'll have none of it!"

"Then stay here."

"Maybe I will."

"Ha! Do you want to be standing here alone when they find you?"

"Shannon . . ."

He lit another candle from the end of his and handed it to her, stuffing the rest into his shirt. "We won't leave any for them." He reached for her hand.

Felicia drew back. "It doesn't look safe."

"We'll take our chances. The thing's been here for centuries. Surely it will last a little longer."

"If you say so." She put her hand in his and stepped through the doorway. A spiderweb clung to her face. She gasped, stifling a scream. Frantically, she wiped her face.

"What is it?"

"There are spiders in here!"

"There were spiders in there, too." He pulled her along.

"Aren't you afraid of them?"

"No."

"I am." She dug in her heels.

"For God's sake, Felicia, what are a few spiders compared to getting out of here?"

"Spiders bite."

"Damme! Aren't a few spiders worth not getting your throat cut?" He sighed with irritation. "Look, I'll go ahead, and you can follow. That way I'll knock down the webs and get bitten by all the spiders."

She took a deep breath. "All right."

Shannon started through the tunnel, and Felicia fell in behind him. The structure looked no safer as they progressed. Crumbling brick and earth had fallen in places, leaving nothing but dirt to support the roof. Tree roots had pushed through, causing them to crawl under them, or climb around. The floor was rough with them and with heaved pavers.

"This is an awful place," Felicia whispered.

"I think it's rather fascinating. When this is over, I'd like to come back here and explore."

"Just like a child!" she hissed and tripped, stumbling against his back.

"Watch where you're going."

"How can I? I can't see."

"Lower your candle and quit looking for spiders. I'm catching them all."

Felicia shuddered and tucked her fingers into his waistband.

He jumped. "What are you doing?"

"Steadying myself."

"How do you expect me to concentrate when you have your hand in my breeches?"

"Don't exaggerate. All I can feel is your shirt."

"It is beyond all decency."

"Yes, it is," she snapped, "and so is this tunnel! Now, my fine, proper lord, what do you wish me to do? Hold onto you in the only place I can, or fall on my face?"

Grumbling, he moved on. "What did I do to deserve this?"

"You initiated it," she fired back.

He didn't reply, and they continued silently through the tunnel. Since the footing was so bad, it was difficult to tell, but it seemed as though the passage had begun a gradual incline. Probably Shannon was right, and it did end at a river, Felicia mused, but there must be something blocking the exit. Escape couldn't be so easy.

Not that this was effortless. Her shoes were not made for traipsing about on rough terrain, and her feet had begun to ache. In fact, she was hurting all over from this churlish treatment. Her lack of food and sleep, combined with her fear, had exhausted her. She didn't know when she had been as miserable as she was at this moment.

Poor Shannon must be feeling much the same. He had suffered all of the horrid experience and, in addition, had been hit hard on the head. The injury must pain him terribly.

Felicia felt ashamed of her own weakness, when Shannon must feel just as afflicted. She still didn't agree entirely with his insistence on escape, but she must admit that he did have a point. She vowed, once more, to be nice to him.

Hearing him swear lightly under his breath, she looked ahead. A very large section of the ceiling had fallen, leaving a pile of debris almost as large as the tunnel itself.

"What shall we do?" she asked.

"I think there's enough room to squeeze through. Wait here."

Heart in her mouth, Felicia watched fearfully as Shannon climbed up the side of the pile. What if it caved in on him? How could she dig him out?

"Come on!" He reached his hand out to her. "We can get through."

Hurriedly she followed him, crawling on her stomach through the narrow opening and rolling down the other side.

"Very good, m'lady." Shannon sprawled against the side of the tunnel and beckoned her down beside him. "I know you climbed trees when you were a little girl. Did you also explore caves?"

"No! And I shall never want to do so again!"

He laughed softly and slipped his arm around her, drawing her to his chest. "You're very tired, aren't you?"

"Yes, as you must be, too." She lay her head against him, closing her eyes.

"You forget. I had a nap!"

"Does your head pain you so terribly much?"

"It hurts enough. It's going away a little."

"I wish I could do something to help."

"You're doing very well just as you are, even though you do like to stop and argue every now and then. I can't think of any lady of the *ton* with whom I'd rather crawl through a tunnel. Can you imagine? Any of them would have fainted long ago."

"Yes." Felicia giggled. "I was never noted for sense or sensibility."

"I think you've sufficient of both. Maybe you sometimes ignore them." He dropped a kiss on her forehead. "Shall we go on?"

"Must we?"

"I'm sorry, love."

Reluctantly she let him help her up. She dreaded the continuation of their journey, but she felt a glowing warmth. He had called her "love" again.

16

THE FOOTING GREW more difficult as Shannon and Felicia progressed. Here the tunnel showed signs of flooding. The brick floor was rugged, and in some places it was entirely washed away or covered with a layer of sandy silt. But this did prove Shannon right. The passage had to lead to a river.

They could smell the water, too. The air, locked into the small corridor with no freshening movement, was heavy with dampness, decay, and the musky odor of fish. That, along with her hunger, made Felicia slightly nauseous and light-headed. She wobbled after Shannon as long as she could, then tugged on his waistband.

"Shannon, I'm sorry. I have to sit down."

"Just keep on a little bit farther. We must be nearly there."

She plopped down on the floor. "I can't."

"We're so close!"

She shook her head, leaning against the side of the tunnel. "If I don't rest, I'm going to fall on my face."

"Very well." He sat down beside her and pillowed her head against his shoulder. "Poor little girl," he said softly, "you must be reaching the end of your strength."

"No! I'll be fine after I've rested awhile." She relaxed against him. "Do you suppose that they've discovered us missing yet?"

"Who's to know?"

"I wonder what time it is ... if they've had time to get to London and back."

"I don't know. They stole my timepiece."

Felicia sighed. "It was valuable, of course."

"It was my father's."

"I'm so sorry."

He shrugged. "I'd rather not have lost it, but I was never particularly close to my father. We were very different from each other. He was so dignified and straitlaced."

She laughed lightly. "I remember that I accused you of being that."

"I suppose you were right."

"No I wasn't. You're not like that at all. Not really. Not inside. You've been trying to act like your father!"

"Felicia, this is ridiculous. I'm not going to sit in this damned tunnel and talk about myself, as though we were having a comfortable coze in your salon. My mind is occupied with getting us out of here, just as any other man's mind would be. Don't you understand anything about men?"

"I'm learning a great deal about one man. Shannon, why are you so touchy?"

"Who wouldn't be? Don't you realize how dangerous this situation is?"

"I'm trying not to!" she wailed.

He hugged her briefly. "I'm sorry. Perhaps I have a great deal to learn about women, too. Go ahead with your conversation. We're going to have to be moving on soon."

Felicia brightened. "We could talk about Penelope."

"Not her again!"

"About the Allerton ball?"

"No!"

"The mob of women who stormed your house?"

"Felicia!"

She giggled. "Have you a suggestion?"

"We could discuss Cousin Theodora," he said wickedly.

"No, we shall not! The one good thing about this situation is that she is not here. I don't want to think about her. Lord, I'll have to face her soon enough, and it will be an awful scene."

"Well, you won't have to put up with her for long. When we're married, you can send her packing."

"Married?" She sat up straight. "No, my lord, I won't force you to that. We've done nothing wrong."

He began to laugh. "Your trouble, Felicia, is that you refuse to face reality. We've done everything wrong."

"No, we haven't. I refuse to talk about this any further." She returned to his shoulder.

"Those men were not wrong when they thought you were Lady Carlington. They were only precipitous."

Felicia felt a warm flush spreading from her neck to her face. She was glad that it was dark enough that he couldn't see it. Deny it though she must, she wished she could be Lady Carlington. It would be heaven to be Shannon's wife, but it couldn't happen. They didn't suit. She would make him miserable with her antics, and probably ruin his reputation, as well as his political chances. And furthermore, she would never, *ever* marry a man who thought he *had* to marry her. The man she would wed would think her the most wonderful woman he'd ever known.

She cleared away the lump in her throat. "What are we going to do if we get out of here? We've no money. How are we going to get back to London?"

"Walk?"

She had to laugh at that. "I can see us now! Lord Shannon Carlington and Lady Felicia Harding walking along the road like two of the most wretched vagrants! I suppose that's how we look," she said ruefully. "I'm glad it's dark so that I can't see the filth."

He chuckled. "First we'll try to find some kind soul to give us some food. Then we'll find out where we are and proceed from there. Now, we'd better be on our way."

"Just a few more minutes? Please?"

"Felicia, we must . . ." He shook his head. "All right. You rest for a few more minutes, but I'm going up ahead. I think we're nearly at the end. I'll be back for you."

She nodded numbly, not wishing to be alone, but coveting the extra respite. Leaning once again against the side of the tunnel, she heard his footsteps disappearing until there was silence. Loneliness settled over her. The few more minutes rest weren't as pleasurable as she had thought they would be. Not without him. Resolutely, she stood up and shook the dirt from her skirt. Shannon couldn't be that far ahead. She would follow him.

She took an uncertain step on the rough terrain and paused, holding her breath. Had she heard a voice? Ears straining, she waited for the next muffled sound. It *was* a voice! It was very far away, but it was unmistakable. The men must have discovered their absence and were coming after them.

Felicia waited no longer. Heart in her throat, she plunged through the corridor, hoping that her soft shoes would be unheard. How far had Shannon gone? She wished she could scream for him, but she knew that a cry would only bring their captors that much more quickly. Perhaps they still had a chance, especially if the end of the passageway was as close as Shannon seemed to think.

Hurtling along so fast that her single candle could do little to illuminate the way, she stumbled on a jagged rising of brick and fell headlong, sliding on her elbows and forearms along the floor. The force of her fall knocked the wind out of her. Gasping for breath, she struggled to a sitting position as her taper snuffed out on the damp ground.

Flashes of pain shot up her leg from her throbbing ankle. Mentally cursing and trying unsuccessfully to hold back the tears, she grasped the injured ankle. It was swelling rapidly. Already it seemed to cause her shoe to pinch, but she had to go on. She couldn't wait helplessly and let them find her here. They had come so far in this hellish place. She couldn't stop now.

Using the tunnel wall as a prop, Felicia forced herself up onto her good leg and gingerly tried to take a step. The damaged ankle gave way and she found herself on the ground again. Where was Shannon? If she could only lean against him!

Rising to her hands and knees, she began to crawl. In the darkness it was difficult to find her way, and she continually bumped against the sides. Sharp snags of brick cut the palms of her hands and her knees. After a very short way, she was forced to stop.

This was ridiculous. She was succeeding in doing nothing but abrading her body terribly in order to gain only a few short yards. She couldn't go on. They would find her here, and who knew what they might do to her?

Her ankle bursting with pain, Felicia collapsed onto the floor and lay her head on her arm. "Shannon!" she sobbed.

Tom Rawlings, the leader of the band of cutthroats, felt no great satisfaction in having throttled Mullins and his idiot brother, nor in blackening the good eye of One-Eyed Jed. It wasn't their fault that the fancy earl and his lady had decided to go exploring. He thought he'd hit Lord Carlington hard enough to keep him on his back for as long as was necessary to implement The Plan, but apparently the nob was tougher than he thought. At least the couple couldn't escape. Rawlings knew these ruins like he knew the back of his hand. Carlington could wander all he wanted, but the only way out was through the sturdy oak door.

"Would've thought we'd come on 'em by now," Jed whined, reaching up to touch the swelling flesh around his eye.

"Shut up! I've had enough of you!"

"Who'd 'ave thought they'd bolt?"

"Yes, and who'd have thought that Mr. Prissy Secretary of Carlington's would've wanted more proof?" He stumbled. "Hold up that damn lantern!"

"What're you gonna do, Tom?" another voice chimed in.

"I'm gonna take locks of hair."

"It's a trap," Jed said suddenly. "They put you off so's they could follow you."

"No, they didn't. We doubled back and watched. They didn't do nothing. They're afraid we'll hurt their lord 'n' lady." He tripped again.

"I'd like to hurt 'em! This time they get tied up, and they stay that way!"

"Even the lady?"

"Especially her! His Lordship's got enough sense to follow orders. That little vixen'd sooner claw yer eyes out as look at you. I'd like to turn her over m'knee and whip her black and blue. No wonder that secretary showed more interest in gettin' the earl back than he did in her."

Rawlings paused, leaning against the side of the tunnel to catch his breath. Too much ale and too much greasy bacon had taken its toll on his middle-aged midsection. It had been a long time since any of his nefarious plans had included a long and difficult hike.

"Maybe she ain't 'is lady. Maybe she's 'is doxy."

"Who'd want a doxy with a temper like that?" He pushed himself up and started on. "Don't matter anyway. I priced 'em two for one."

Shannon hesitated, listening. Had he heard Felicia's voice? Surely not. Hadn't he told her he'd return for her? She couldn't be so foolish as to call for him, when the men could be following them at this very moment, unless . . . unless she was in trouble.

"Shannon . . . Shannon, help me."

He bounded back in the direction he had come, panic rising in his throat. Dear God, what could be wrong? If something had happened to her, he would never forgive himself. He should never have left her alone.

The corridor was dark as far as he could see. Perhaps her candle had gone out, frightening her. That could badly scare a woman in such a situation. He hoped that it was nothing more.

He stopped and listened again. "Felicia?" he whispered loudly.

"Shannon! I see you!" she cried softly. "I'm here."

Lifting the candle to better illuminate the tunnel, he hurried forward and found her lying on the floor. "Darling! What . . ."

"The men!" she hissed tearfully. "I heard their voices."

"Then we've got to run for it." He stooped to help her up. "I haven't found the end, but it's got to be just ahead. Come on!"

"I can't!" she sobbed. "I've hurt myself."

He swore lightly under his breath. "What . . ."

"It's my ankle. I was running to you . . . and I fell. Shannon, if I could just lean on you, I can walk. I know I can!"

His mind raced. "How close do you think the men were?"

"I don't know! They sounded very far away." She clutched his arm. "Help me up. I can do it."

"It would be too slow." He handed her the candle and swooped her up into his arms.

"You can't do this. I'm too heavy!"

"Shh."

"Shannon, I'm so sorry. If it hadn't been for me . . ."

"Shut up, Felicia, and let me get you out of this tangle." He began walking as quickly as he could toward what had to be the opening of the passageway.

"I will never, ever disobey anyone again. I shall be circumspect . . ."

"No you won't. When you're seventy years old, you'll still be a hoyden. I shall obtain peace only through death."

"You will obtain peace, my lord, as soon as I am

restored to my father," she said archly, "for I shall never marry you."

"We'll see about that. Now, shut up! Do you want those men to hear you?"

He was surprised that she fell silent without having the final say. The fear, the discomfort, and the pain from her ankle must be taking their toll on her willfulness. He stopped to shift his delicate burden and, from a distance, heard the sound of tramping feet.

Felicia stiffened in his arms. "They're coming."

Shannon quickened his pace, half running on the uneven ground.

"Do be careful!" Felicia cried softly.

"I'm trying!"

The passageway slanted downwards. Stopping in his tracks, Shannon saw why their abductors hadn't seemed concerned about their escape. The tunnel ended in a small room filled with water.

Felicia slumped in his arms. "It's no use."

His own spirits plummeted. What horrid luck to have their difficult wanderings end in this. The river had risen, or changed its course, and had backed up into the ruins.

He set her down carefully and lifted the candle to illuminate the chamber. On the opposite side he could see the top of an archway leading from it. There were only inches separating the top of the arch from the water, but through it there seemed to be a sliver of light.

"Felicia, can you swim?"

"Dear God, Shannon, don't you know when we are defeated?"

"We aren't defeated yet," he said stubbornly. "Can you swim?"

"Not very well, and with my ankle . . ."

"Can you hold your breath and cling to me?"

"If I must."

"All right." He picked her up again and walked down the incline. Briefly touching his lips to hers, he eased her down into the water.

"It's cold." Felicia's teeth chattered.

"You'll get used to it in a moment." He stuck the candle upright between the bricks and plunged in beside her. "Hold tight," he warned and struck out swimming toward the archway.

Felicia tucked her hand securely into his waistband, and with her other arm gamely made swimming strokes. She managed to kick a little with her uninjured leg.

"Good girl," Shannon said approvingly, again awed by her tenacity. No woman he had ever met could have made it this far. She had to be the most unusual young lady in England, if not the world. Her gentle upbringing could never have prepared her for what she had gone through last night and today. She would have made a good soldier's wife, following the troops with nary a complaint. Suddenly he wanted very much to marry her, whether he had to or not.

They reached the wall. Shannon caught the top of the arch and steadied himself, treading water. "Now is the time to hold your breath, darling."

"How do we know that this doesn't lead to just another water-logged room?"

"We've come this far. We have to try. You see, there's a bit of space between the water and the ceiling. If we run out of air we can turn on our backs and lift our noses up. You jerk hard on my waistband if you need to do that." Glancing back, he saw a lantern bobbing in the distance. "Now! They're almost here!"

He caught her shoulders and ducked under, taking her with him. With his other hand he reached up to the roof of the archway and pulled them hastily along. He prayed there wouldn't be a door to block their progress.

In a very short time he touched the last foot of rough stone and felt only air on his hand. Heart pounding, he surfaced, dragging her after him. Sunlight blazed in his eyes. He felt near amazement to see the wide river with its tree-studded banks.

"We did it!" Felicia gasped, throwing her arms around his neck. "Oh Shannon, you are so wonderful!"

He hugged her, grinning.

"I knew you would take care of me!"

"You must give yourself some of the credit. I doubt that any other woman could have done what you have done." He kissed her nose. "But we aren't safe yet. We don't want them to find us on the shore. We'll swim a little way with the current."

"It's a big river."

"I wouldn't be surprised if it were the Thames."

"Perhaps we should try to cross to the opposite side."

"I intend to . . . a ways down from where we are, so we won't make such a target. I hope they'll think we've got out on shore, and that we're somewhere on the grounds. We'll swim down below that bend, so we'll have some cover."

"Anything you say."

He slipped his arm around her waist and struck out with a powerful side stroke. At this rate of speed, they should be around the bend before the men were able to backtrack and come looking for them on the shore. Now there only remained the problem of finding something to eat and traveling back to London, without any money. From the way he must look, he doubted that anyone would believe that he was the wealthy Earl of Carlington.

17

LORD TORRENCE SAW the horses held by a gangly youth in the otherwise empty courtyard and drew back into the fringe of the trees. "Surround the place," he ordered his motley army. "Do it quietly, and stay out of sight. When I raise my arm, we shall attack." He glanced at Lord Favoringham for approval.

The duke frowned. "Perhaps we should make an offer. I want my daughter back safe and sound, as you, of course, want Lord Carlington. That is more important than catching those scoundrels. If we make a fight of it, they have nothing to lose. They might kill them!"

Torrence considered. Favoringham was probably right. If their army of servants caught them—and they would, for they vastly outnumbered the brigands—the kidnappers would surely swing at Tyburn. For spite, they just might kill Shannon and the Lady Felicia.

But he didn't like the idea of negotiating with criminals. In the first place they were dishonest, or they wouldn't be the bunch of malefactors that they were. They could take his and Favoringham's money and still hold their prisoners hostage. Where would it all end?

Secondly, the kidnappers might be bold enough to try it again. Some other poor unsuspecting soul might fall prey to their trap. As a high peer of the Realm, and a respected member of the House of Lords, Torrence must set aside his own emotions and act for the general good of the people. It was his responsibility.

The lawbreakers were the scum of the earth. It was within his power to put a period to their depredations. Wellington wouldn't have hesitated. Shannon himself, if the dispatches were to be believed, would have gone for the throat. No, he mustn't be swayed by the personal element. They must rid England of this blight.

"I believe," he said cautiously, "that we should swoop down upon them, taking them by surprise. It is our duty as honorable men to see that these acts do not continue."

Favoringham swore loudly, causing the lad holding the horses to look toward the woods. "Dammit, Torrence, who do you think you are? Some damn Crusader? I want my little girl, and I want her alive. I'll not listen to this patriotic poppycock!"

"Excellent, Your Grace! Now they know we're here."

"They know nothing. Do you see that fellow running to tell? No!"

Torrence shifted nervously in the saddle. "Keep your voice down."

"I'll tell you a thing or two, my impudent young duke. I shall be in charge here! Your family has gotten us into this tangle, and it is up to me to get us out!"

"*My* family!"

"Yes, *your* family! I have had nothing but trouble since your brother-in-law made the acquaintance of my daughter!" Favoringham snapped. "Oh, don't get me wrong. I am well enough angry with Felicia, but she wouldn't be here today without the influence of Carlington!"

"I beg to disagree." Torrence firmly pressed his lips together.

"Disagree all you like. What is true is true. I am going now to treat with those men and obtain the release of my daughter. You can do what you like about your brother."

"Brother-in-law," the duke said forcefully. "And this is how I'll treat with them!" Signaling his army, he spurred forward, brandishing his pistol.

Shots rang out as the excited servants launched their attack. Unarmed, the youth in the courtyard foolishly stared at the onslaught, as the horses he was holding pitched and reared, breaking free and clattering wildly across the cobblestones. Torrence skirted a gelding that had caught his foot in the dangling reins and somersaulted in front of him. Turning the shoulder of his horse into the awed boy, he knocked him down and drew rein. Favoringham's animal plunged into his from the rear, nearly sending the young duke flying over his mount's ears.

"Where are they?" he shouted to the lad, righting himself and favoring Felicia's father with a grimace.

The youth merely gazed admiringly at the lord.

"Where are they, I say?"

"He's a half-wit. Must be a relative of yours, Torrence." Lord Favoringham shoved forward. "Boy, where are your friends? And the lady and gentleman?"

"Pretty lady ran away."

"Where? Where did she run, where are the others?"

"Tunnel."

Torrence dismounted. "Take us there."

The boy glanced uncertainly at Lord Favoringham.

"Yes." The old duke nodded firmly. "You will show us where the pretty lady went."

"Like to see pretty lady again."

"So you shall. If you help us, you shall be rewarded."

Torrence groaned.

"Yes, now here we go." Favoringham propelled him toward the priory with Torrence and the army quickly following.

Hearing gunshots, Shannon stopped swimming and drew Felicia close. "Did you hear that?"

"They're coming after us!" she cried. "They're going to kill us!"

"I don't think so. They haven't had time to get out of the tunnel yet. And I could swear that I heard Edward's voice."

"Who is that?"

"Torrence. My brother-in-law."

"It is impossible! How could they know where we are?"

"I don't know. Shh . . ." He tread water, listening. In the distance he could hear voices and the milling of shod horses on stone. "I think we have a rescue party. Come on." He started toward the bank.

"Shannon, wait! What if it isn't?"

"It is." He drew her after him, giving her little choice but to move with him.

"But what if my father is there?"

"You must face him sometime."

She pulled back, jerking him upright. "I'm not ready to!"

"Then stay in the river." He let go her waist.

"Shannon!" Felicia floundered, taking in a great gulp of river water and coughing wildly.

He caught her once more. "Darling, I am tired and hungry. My head is bursting. We don't know what is wrong with your ankle. I'm not looking forward to facing them either, least of all your father, but it must be done!"

"Yes, Shannon." She meekly touched the lump on his head. "I am selfish . . . when you have been so brave, and . . ."

Without waiting for her to finish, he swam to shore, pulled her up onto the bank, and dropped down beside her. "Well, we are a bit cleaner."

It was the only compliment he could have given her. Never had he seen a woman of quality look so tousled, bedraggled, and uninspiring. Even the plain, square-jawed Lady Penelope could have outshone Felicia at the moment. Her tangled hair had lost all its pins and dripped over her face and down her back in long, stringy ropes. Her dress, luckily not torn at the bodice, was frayed at the hem and split at the knees. Despite the soaking in the river, a smudge of dirt remained on her nose and on one of her delicate cheekbones. He grinned.

"Just what do you find so amusing?" she demanded, sitting up.

"You. You look awful."

"You don't look so fine yourself, Shannon Carlington!" she snapped. "No doubt your own condition is most offensive to your high sense of fastidiousness and decency."

He glanced down at his attire. His white silk shirt had turned a dingy beige and had lost several of its buttons, exposing an alarming amount of muscular chest. His once-shining Hessians were ruined beyond reclamation; his valet would throw them out with the trash. His cravat was missing entirely. The landlord at the inn on Hounslow Heath was probably wearing his perfect Weston coat.

Felicia began to laugh. "No one would believe it! My lord, I doubt that you even dipped so low when you rode with Wellington. You look as though you've spent the night in the gutter outside a gin shop."

At least she was returning to normal again. But what was normal for Felicia? She could change moods quicker than any woman he had ever known.

He stood and bent down to pick her up. "Let us go and be rescued."

"Let me try to walk again. After the cold water, my ankle is feeling ever so much better."

"It's not a good idea. Wait until a physician sees it."

"I don't like physicians," she quarreled. "They're all quacks."

He gathered her up and impulsively kissed her. "Thank you for being a good sport through all of this. It would have been impossible if you hadn't."

"Why, Shannon! A compliment?"

"You know you deserve it." He chuckled and started into the trees.

Felicia tilted back her head and gazed up at him flirtatiously. "Under ordinary circumstances, it is expected that a lady thank a gentleman for the entertainment he has provided her. In this case, however, I believe I shall forego it . . . though it did have its moments!" She sighed, sobering. "If I only didn't have to face Papa. Ugh! And Cousin Theodora, too."

Shannon silently agreed. He would rather do

most anything than face Lord Favoringham, let alone Cousin Theodora. He would assure the duke, as quickly as possible, that he would marry his daughter. At least that would take some of the sting out of it.

Nearing the edge of the woods, he deposited Felicia under a massive oak and went on alone to make sure that the commotion was indeed caused by a rescue party. Immediately, he spotted the quality horses, familiar faces, and a coach bearing the arms of Lord Favoringham. In the center of the activity was the heavily trussed and guarded band of brigands. Nodding to himself, he returned for Felicia.

"It is as I suspected. A rescue party has arrived from London, and the men are captured."

"Is Papa . . ."

"Yes, I saw your father among them." He saw her pinched expression and touched her cheek. "Don't worry so. Everything will be all right."

"I hope so," she stammered.

"It will be. Trust me again?" Smiling confidently, he reached down for her.

Felicia slipped her arms around his neck to ease his lifting her. But she knew that this time Shannon was wrong. It would not be all right. Nothing would ever be right again.

He would offer for her like the gentleman he was, her father would accept, Cousin Theodora would be in raptures, but she would hold fast to her resolve of letting him go. None of them could force her to wed a man who didn't love her, and whose life would be made miserable because of her. She could never be the wife that Shannon wanted, even if she tried. She didn't want to be the kind of woman who faded into her husband's shadow. She couldn't imagine being like that namby-pamby nonentity, Penelope Hampstead. Apparently, Shannon wasn't interested in that little prig now, but he had once singled her out for his attention. He must want that type of wife.

No, she wouldn't marry him. It would hurt to say good-bye. But it would hurt much more to see his disappointment and his anger every day for the rest of her life.

Her refusal would mean banishment from Society forever. The *ton* would never forget such a scandal. They would always speculate about her conduct during the long hours she had spent alone with him.

For a while Shannon would suffer the gossip, but he would soon be forgiven. After all, he was a man and a prize catch on the Marriage Mart. Only the highest sticklers would censure him for long. Mamas with eligible daughters wouldn't bat an eye. They would all blame her.

A choking sensation rose in her throat, making her wish she could weep to relieve it. This was the last time she would be in Shannon's arms. Probably within the year, he would belong to someone else. She hoped that the lady who married him would stand up to him now and then, to keep his overbearing masculinity in check.

A shout reached her ears. "There they are!" She turned her face into his chest.

"It will be all right," he murmured again, encouragingly.

"Felicia!" It was her father's voice.

Taking a deep breath she raised her head and looked at him through a blur of tears.

"Daughter, are you all right?" He started to take her from Shannon's arms, but the earl refused to relinquish his burden.

"Lady Felicia has hurt her ankle, Your Grace. Allow me to carry her to the coach."

Hearing Shannon slip back so easily to formal address overset Felicia even further. Tears flowed down her cheeks. Her throat seemed full to the bursting point.

Lord Favoringham skipped alongside like a worrisome puppy. "Other than that, is she all right?"

"Yes, sir."

Shannon entered the coach with her and laid her on the seat, covering her with a soft carriage robe.

Felicia smiled tremulously. "You don't know how good this feels. You should do the same."

"Now that would be pretty behavior." He grinned.

"But your head . . . You must not forget it."

"I won't. It won't let me."

"My lord," the Duke of Favoringham said impatiently. "Permit me to tend my daughter."

"Yes, sir." He squeezed her hand and backed out. "Caring for her has become a habit."

"I am glad that you consider it as such," Felicia's father said coldly, "for you will be doing it for a very long time."

"Of course, sir."

"Torrence assured me that you would do the honorable thing."

"I will do it with pleasure," Shannon said quietly. "Indeed, I am the one who will be honored by the gift of your daughter's hand."

"Prettily said, Carlington."

Felicia's cheeks burned. How could they stand there so politely agreeing upon the future, when the present hadn't even been addressed? Tears evaporating, she frowned heavily at her father as he stepped into the carriage and took the seat opposite.

"Papa, you are appalling beyond belief! How can you stand there muttering inanities? We have been through a terrible ordeal. Can you not have the simple decency to see to our comfort before you begin your attempt to manipulate us to do your will?"

"I had to be sure," he growled. "This time, Felicia, you have really landed in the suds. What do you have to say for yourself?"

"I am tired, and I am hungry, and my ankle hurts. That is all I have to say at present."

"Did you deliberately set out to trap that man?"

"I set out to free myself of Cousin Theodora! Lord Carlington was kind and understanding enough to see my plight and to wish to help me."

"For your sake, I hope he remains kind and understanding. For my own, I'd rather see him turn you over his knee every morning and beat you black and blue! Really, Felicia, how could you ever come up with such a scandalous scheme? Have you no thought at all for your reputation?"

She drew herself up to a sitting position. "It would have worked."

"Fustian! You silly goose, don't you know that there is always someone who will observe and tell?"

"I was desperate."

"Then you should have come to me."

"How can you say that?" she cried. "I did come to you, Papa, and you would only agree to impracticalities! I tried to come to you again, but you deliberately avoided me!"

"I would never do such a thing."

"Yes, you did! You most certainly did!"

Lord Favoringham mopped his forehead with a

pristine white handkerchief. "I am a busy man. You should have had patience."

"Fiddlesticks."

"You may believe what you wish, Felicia, but you are wrong. Perhaps I was in error by allowing Cousin Theodora to remain, but you must admit that you needed guidance. So I was wrong! But, my dear, you must admit that I have always had your best interests at heart."

"I know," she sighed, lying back again, "but you quit listening to me, Papa. Ever since that episode at Carlington House, you have refused to try to understand my side of things. Andrew wouldn't help. He is too fearful of losing his allowance. I had to rely on myself. I don't believe that my solution was irrational. If all had gone as planned, I would be at home in the country. Few would be the wiser as to how I got there."

He shook his head. "The truth would have come out, sooner or later."

"No one could have proved it!"

"Ah well, I shan't fence with you any longer. Carlington will soon have the governing of you. Perhaps a younger man will have better luck."

"No, Papa. I shall not marry Shannon Carlington."

He stared at her, thunderstruck. "Felicia, you must! After what has happened?"

"No." Again the tears began to trickle down her cheeks.

"He will make you a good husband!"

"I know."

"Then why . . ."

"I won't marry him because I love him!" she sobbed. "I won't do it to him! He doesn't want the kind of wife I would be. I will go to the country and never leave it. Then I will no longer be a bother or an embarrassment to anyone."

"Felicia . . . my dear!"

"I won't, and no one can force me!"

Looking as though he himself had been through the kidnapping ordeal instead of his daughter, Lord Favoringham patted her hand. "There now . . . I'm going to see that you get food and drink. After that you'll feel more the thing."

"Yes," she choked, "I probably will, but I won't change my mind. I shall not marry Shannon."

Shaking his head, he backed out of the carriage.

"Papa?"

"Yes, my dear?"

"There was a lackwit among those men, who was kind to me. He brought me a blanket. Please see that he isn't treated as harshly as the others. It isn't his fault that he has fallen among these cutthroats."

"It will be done. But, Felicia, about the other matter . . ."

She closed her eyes. "Nothing will change my mind."

Muttering to himself, Lord Favoringham turned back into the courtyard. Women! How could she be so thoughtless of her own future, and so caring of that of one of her captors? He had never understood his daughter. He would never understand her.

18

LORD TORRENCE DREW his brother-in-law some distance away from the others and turned to face him. "Well, Shannon, do you care to tell me what is going on?"

Shannon looked into the duke's hazel eyes, seeing a strange mixture of anger, curiosity, and disgust. Edward was definitely not in good humor, nor was he likely to prove a sympathetic audience. He had the sudden sensation that the day his sister's husband had agreed with him over the matter of Lady Penelope would never repeat itself.

"Let's not do this now, Edward. It isn't a good time."

"You'll agree to marry her?"

"I have already done so."

He shook his head sadly. "What a waste."

"What do you mean by that?" Shannon asked sharply. He knew his family was going to be displeased by the culmination of his folly, but there was no other way for him to resolve the dilemma. Nor did he wish there to be.

"Your career in the government!" the duke said impatiently. "When this scandal is bruited about, no one will take you seriously. Also, from what I understand, your countess will do you little credit."

Shannon's throbbing head did nothing to aid him in keeping his temper. "I care little what you understand, Edward. I am marrying Felicia Harding because I *want* to, not because I *have* to."

"Admirable, I'm sure. An attitude like that will ease the loss of your career."

"And as far as the House of Lords is concerned, no one there ever took me seriously in the first place. Or you, for that matter! Tories with Whig sentiments, that's all anyone ever noticed! If anything is a waste, it is the House of Lords. It's a big waste of time. I'll be in my grave before the government offers anything but rhetoric to improve the social conditions of this country. I'd do better to establish my own social programs, with my own money."

"Don't be ridiculous."

"I am not. Edward, can't this wait till later?"

"Are you aware that you have given much grief and concern to Eliza and Lady Carlington?"

"Yes," he said wearily.

"Do you also realize that your reactions will affect us all for a very long time?"

Shannon gritted his teeth. "No, I don't agree with that. What has happened concerns only myself and Felicia. There will be talk, of course, but I'm sure you will handle it with your usual aplomb. No one will blame any of you. Indeed, they will probably pity you for having such a black sheep for a brother-in-law. Cut line, Edward! You're scolding me as if I were a recalcitrant schoolboy."

"That is how you have conducted yourself. Shannon, will you never learn to behave with responsibility? With propriety?"

"Apparently not." He turned on his heel and left Lord Torrence standing alone and angry on the fringe of the woods.

Returning to the courtyard, he gave a half-smile to Ev, Marcus, and Tom, who were lounging on a low wall and enjoying the bottle of brandy they were passing back and forth.

They motioned to him. "Trouble with Torrence, Shan?" Marcus asked.

"Are you surprised?"

He shook his head and handed the bottle to his friend. "Sorry we had to bring him in on this, but he had to know."

"You told him?" He took a long, satisfying drink of the liquor, feeling its numbing warmth ease his hunger and his temper. "How did you three become involved?"

"We followed you and Lady Felicia out of London. Had nothing better to do! And our curiosity was piqued by what you'd told us at White's the other night. You were very protective of the lady. Most unusual, I thought."

"Yes, Marcus, you were always able to see through subterfuge. You should have been a spy during the war." Shannon laughed shortly, drinking deeply again and handing back the bottle. "So the three of you were at the inn?"

"Yes, in the barn across the road. There was nothing we could do. Being unprepared for a jaunt across Hounslow, we were unarmed. We followed you here, then went for help."

"Thank you! I am in your debt."

"No." The young earl shook his head. "This whole unfortunate episode is really our fault. If we hadn't . . . Well, there's no point crying over spilt milk. It won't happen again, not to you or to anyone. We'll never play another prank."

"Learned your lesson, eh?" Shannon laughed. "I'm glad you didn't learn it before I met Felicia. If it hadn't been for you, I'd never have paid the slightest heed to her. She's a very special lady, you know."

"You're in love with her," Ev perceived.

"Exactly."

"Then you won't mind marrying her?" Tom asked cautiously.

"I'll be delighted."

Marcus heaved a sigh. "All will be well. Congratulations, Shan." He passed the brandy to his friend. "She's a lucky lady."

"I'm the lucky one. I couldn't ask for a more perfect wife."

His three friends slipped from the wall as the men began to mount up. "It seems we're off for London."

Shannon's stomach rolled. "Hasn't anyone anything to eat?"

"Your fiancée. Someone put a basket of food in the carriage," Marcus said pointedly. "You should ride with her anyway. Your head looks nasty, in addition to the fact that her company would be much more enjoyable," he added slyly.

"Yes it would, wouldn't it?" Shannon grinned and strode toward the Favoringham coach, to be met halfway by Felicia's father.

"You've got to talk some sense into her head, Carlington. The chit's full of female foolishness! Says she won't marry you!"

"She will."

"Don't be so sure. The gel's hard-headed as they come! I never could control her. Maybe you'll have better luck," Favoringham muttered. "I was going to ride back to town with the both of you. As chaperon, don't you know! Now it's best you ride alone with her. Court her a bit, cuddle her . . ." He feverishly wiped his brow. "Who am I to give advice? It's never worked!"

"Leave it to me," Shannon assured with a confidence he didn't feel.

"I'm depending upon you." He caught Shannon's elbow to hurry him along. "And I want you to know that I think you'll be a good son-in-law. I'll be glad to have you in the family."

"Thank you, sir."

"Damn it all! What'll I do if she won't accept?" Fretfully, the Duke of Favoringham wandered off toward his horse, as Shannon stepped into the carriage.

Felicia was sound asleep, curled up on the seat with the blanket drawn cozily around her. He didn't have the heart to wake her. She'd been his partner in more than most ladies could bear. Right now she needed her rest. Sitting down opposite, he finished the ample remains of the lunch and stretched out, letting the gentle rocking of Lord Favoringham's well-sprung coach lull him to slumber.

It was late when the carriage pulled to a stop in front of Carlington House. Felicia awoke, slightly rested, but still exhausted. Sitting up, she looked at the sleeping form across from her and touched his shoulder. "Shannon, we are in London. Here is your house."

Yawning, he pushed himself up and grinned at her. "I haven't been much company."

The yawn was contagious. "Neither have I."

"I'll see you in the morning."

"It isn't necessary."

"Oh, yes, Felicia. You know it is." He got up,

pausing to place a light kiss on her lips. "Good night, darling."

Even the quick, casual kiss from him had the power to send her senses reeling. She pressed her eyelids close together to discourage gathering tears and rested her head against the squabs. She must refuse to see him tomorrow morning, or ever. To see him was to reach out desperately for his embrace. It must never happen again.

Quickly she leaned forward to take one last look at him. He and his brother-in-law were walking up the steps to Carlington House. Apparently they were exchanging some harsh words, for both of them seemed rather irritated. They were probably talking about her. That straightlaced Torrence wouldn't want her in the family. That was another reason why she would be miserable if she were Shannon's wife.

"Well!" Her father took Shannon's place on the opposite seat. "Are you convinced now that you must wed each other?" he asked, smiling like a cat satiated with cream.

"I have already told you how I feel about that."

"But . . ."

"There will be no more discussion," Felicia said firmly. "When we arrive home, I am going to bed. I shall see or talk to no one tomorrow, not even you. And, Father, if you do not keep Cousin Theodora away from me, I shall run away again. If I must do it once again, I shall go where you'll never find me!"

"You must reconsider, Felicia," he said quietly. "You love Carlington, and I believe he loves you."

She clenched her jaw. "Never!" she snapped.

* * *

"Felicia," Andrew begged. "You must come down. Lord Carlington and his whole family are here!"

"Father's war council." She laughed cynically, watching in the mirror as Mary tucked the last lock of hair into her flattering Grecian updo. "There! Now isn't that better than Cousin Theodora's mode?"

"You look like a darling," Andrew murmured, "but don't distract me. You must come down!"

"I will not." She adjusted the shoulders of her blue silk gown.

"Father has instructed me to bring you by force if necessary."

Her answer was a hollow laugh.

"If I do not fetch you immediately, he has threatened to cut off my allowance!"

Felicia eyed him warily. Her brother would move mountains to keep his allowance. He would have her downstairs if he had to sling her over his shoulder like a sack of meal.

She sighed. "Very well, Andrew. I shall come, but it will do no good. I won't marry him."

"For heaven's sake, why not?"

"We wouldn't suit," she said primly.

"Balderdash! I saw the way you looked at each other yesterday! You're in love with him, Felicia, and he with you. Besides, after what happened . . ."

"I will not be forced, Andrew! Don't you realize how miserable we both would be? We are far too different. We would never be compatible."

"I think you complement each other."

"Who cares what you think, Andrew? I assure you that *I* have never done so!" She rose. "I'll be along shortly. Now go on about your business."

Her brother set his jaw. "You, Lady Sister, are

my business, and you are coming with me now," he said firmly, offering his arm.

Felicia had no choice but to allow him to escort her down the stairs. "There is going to be a scene, Andrew," she warned as they entered the parlor. "You won't like it above half."

As Andrew bowed and left her, she became immediately aware of Lady Carlington's presence first. Sitting regally in the largest chair in the room, she seemed to freeze the atmosphere with the cold disapproval in her eyes and in the set of her mouth. On one side sat her daughter, Lady Eliza, looking tearful and unhappy. On the other sat Cousin Theodora, her own features aping the countess' displeasure. By the sideboard, sharing a drink, stood the men, Lord Torrence with stiff forbearance, her father, whose darting eyes betrayed his anxiety, and Shannon, who gave a small shrug and moved forward to take her hands.

"You have nearly recovered, my lady?" he asked politely. "You seem to be walking with only a slight limp."

"I am all right." Her eyes quickly glanced at his head. The wound had been properly cleaned, leaving only the cut and a pinkish stain in his hair to bear witness to what had happened. "And you, my lord?"

"I'm fine." He squeezed her hand. "I want you to meet my family." Leading her forward, he made the introductions.

"Well!" Lady Carlington surveyed her with her lorgnette. "So you are to be my daughter-in-law."

"No, ma'am, I am not. It isn't necessary."

"Not . . . necessary . . ." Shock dripped from the countess' voice. "My gel, I have never been acquainted with anything *more* necessary."

"The whole unfortunate episode was my fault

alone. Your son was a proper gentleman at all times," Felicia said with determination. "I shall not ruin his life, for we wouldn't suit."

Lord Favoringham began to protest, but Lady Carlington lifted an imperious hand. "Very thoughtful, my dear, but sadly impossible. The two of you will wed."

"No, we will not."

"You stupid gel!" Cousin Theodora cried angrily. "Have you no thought for your reputation? Of course you will wed! We will agree to nothing else!"

"I shall not speak the vows!"

"Lady Felicia," Eliza began, "you must heed propriety. My mother is right. You must wed. There can be no other solution."

"Oh, yes, there can." She flashed Shannon a brilliant smile. "You can live it down, my lord, and I . . . I shall go to the country. After all, that is where I had intended on going in the first place."

"Excuse me, Mama," Shannon said, and quickly drew Felicia away to the side of the room. "Is there somewhere we can talk together?"

She looked at him hopefully. Perhaps he had an idea of what they could do to get themselves out of this fix. He didn't want her as a wife. He couldn't! "Through here."

They slipped through the glass doors into the conservatory, as a stiff conversation began between the families. The room was less crowded with oversized plants than most areas of its type. The lush specimens were arranged around the walls in pots and hanging baskets. In the center was an attractive set of cushioned garden furniture. In no section could the couple be out of sight of the occupants of the parlor, but they were out of earshot.

Felicia motioned to the door leading to the rear garden. "We could go out there if you like."

"This will be fine." He turned to face her, laying his hands on her shoulders. "I want to thank you for being so considerate of me."

"I fear it isn't doing much good."

"No."

"Even your mother and sister . . . I don't believe they really wish me to marry you, but they are certainly insistent."

"High sticklers!"

"Maybe they are right," she sighed. "The *ton* would certainly agree with them, but a marriage shouldn't be arranged by others. We have done nothing so terribly wrong."

"Don't you want to marry me, Felicia?"

She gazed up into his wonderfully blue eyes. It was her undoing. Memories of their kisses flitted through her mind, bringing a blush to her cheeks.

"Don't you?" he pressed.

"That is an unfair question, Shannon, when you know how you do not wish to marry me," she said quietly.

"What if I did?"

"We wouldn't suit. I would not be the kind of wife you need. A man in the position you seek must have a very proper wife. I've learned a great many lessons these past days, and I don't believe I'll ever again be the hoyden that I was, but I shall always look for fun . . . and amusing company. It wouldn't work."

She moved away from him to stand at the garden door. At this very young age she had ruined her life, but she would not allow this fine man to ruin his to save her. She hated dull and stuffy political gatherings. She doubted that even the greatest statesmen were true to the ideals they boasted of, except maybe Shannon ... but he was special.

He came up behind her, and once more laid his disturbing hands on her shoulders. "What if I told you," he said slowly, "that you are very precious to me? That I don't think that I will ever be very happy unless you choose to be my wife?"

She trembled.

"Felicia, I believe I have been falling in love with you from the moment I saw you hiding behind those draperies in my salon."

She shook her head. "But what about Penelope?"

Shannon exhaled with exasperation. "Why must she always enter our conversations? Why can you not cease accusing me of having a *tendre* for Penelope Hampstead? I saw her only a few times, and I was totally bored on each occasion!"

"Don't cut up at me."

"I don't want to!" He lowered his voice. "I want to make love to you."

Her heart lurched into her throat. "You do?"

"Yes! I want to marry you and to love you, and I want you to love me. Is that such an impossible dream?"

Felicia turned in his arms, her heart in her eyes. She took a deep breath and slipped her arms around his neck. "No."

"You'll marry me?"

"Yes, for I do love you so very, very much."

He drew her closer. "There is no argument about our feelings for each other?"

Felicia looked into his mischievous face. "None at all."

"Then we shall set the date at once?"

"Whenever you wish! But there is one thing I don't like about it."

"Oh?"

She gestured toward the occupants of the parlor. "Our families. They will believe that we have merely knuckled under to their wishes. I don't want to give them that satisfaction. They must know beyond a doubt that we are marrying each other because *we* wish it."

He grinned.

"You have an idea."

"Come here." He led her to the French doors that opened to the parlor.

"What are we going to do?"

"Trust me."

She eyed him dubiously. "That last time I agreed to trust you . . ."

". . . we escaped our captors."

Felicia smiled. "So we did."

"Now, I'm going to do what I've been wanting to do for the past few hours."

"Which is?"

He gathered her into his arms, bringing his lips purposefully down on hers. The kiss, forceful at first, softened as she yielded to him. Sliding her arms around his shoulders and caressing the back of his neck, Felicia forgot about their families, the visibility of their position in front of the doors, and the propriety of their actions. She thought only of the wonderful man who said he loved her and was proving it so very deliciously.

"Isn't someone going to stop that disgusting display?" Cousin Theodora cried, fumbling for her vinaigrette. "Really, Favoringham, you must put a period to it!"

"And risk Felicia's anger? I think not." He smiled contentedly at the couple.

"This is not your daughter's doing!" Theodora

persisted. "It is that . . . that *man!* Little Felicia would only be too glad of your rescue!"

"Don't look like it to me," Andrew commented.

Cousin Theodora flew at Lady Carlington. "Your son's behavior has gone beyond the pale, madam!"

"It is not *his* conduct!" the dowager shrieked. "That poor gel has been throwing herself at his head ever since she first laid eyes on him!" She turned to her daughter. "I cannot bear that horrid old maid! It is no wonder that Shannon would wish to help Felicia! The sooner we can remove her from that virago's company, the better!"

"I don't think that Shannon wants to wait very long either, Mama," Eliza smiled. "Isn't it romantic? She is so pretty! Won't we have fun shopping with her?"

Torrence caught Favoringham's eye and nodded. "I believe we've all been wasting our breath. Those two want to marry, despite the necessity of it."

"Very well!" Cousin Theodora screeched. "But won't someone stop that Vauxhall Gardens behavior?"

Shannon lifted his head to look down fondly on his betrothed. "I do believe we've made our point."

"So soon?" Felicia asked wistfully.

"Yes." He grinned apologetically. "I intend to run right out to obtain a special license. We shall be married by this time tomorrow."

"That will be wonderful," she cried happily, then sobered. "There is one thing, Shannon. I must promise to obey you, mustn't I?"

"It is part of the marriage vows."

"Hm . . ." She brightened. "If you often kiss me like that, I don't believe I'll mind at all."

"Love, I intend to kiss you very frequently and very thoroughly. Like this?"

He drew her lovingly to his heart, bringing his lips to hers again to seal the bargain.

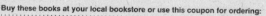

Avon Romances—
the best in exceptional authors and unforgettable novels!

LORD OF MY HEART Jo Beverley
76784-8/$4.50 US/$5.50 Can

BLUE MOON BAYOU Katherine Compton
76412-1/$4.50 US/$5.50 Can

SILVER FLAME Hannah Howell
76504-7/$4.50 US/$5.50 Can

TAMING KATE Eugenia Riley
76475-X/$4.50 US/$5.50 Can

THE LION'S DAUGHTER Loretta Chase
76647-7/$4.50 US/$5.50 Can

CAPTAIN OF MY HEART Danelle Harmon
76676-0/$4.50 US/$5.50 Can

BELOVED INTRUDER Joan Van Nuys
76476-8/$4.50 US/$5.50 Can

SURRENDER TO THE FURY Cara Miles
76452-0/$4.50 US/$5.50 Can

Coming Soon

SCARLET KISSES Patricia Camden
76825-9/$4.50 US/$5.50 Can

WILDSTAR Nicole Jordan
76622-1/$4.50 US/$5.50 Can

Avon Romantic Treasures

*Unforgettable, enthralling love stories,
sparkling with passion and adventure
from Romance's bestselling authors*

ONLY IN YOUR ARMS *by Lisa Kleypas*
76150-5/$4.50 US/$5.50 Can

LADY LEGEND *by Deborah Camp*
76735-X/$4.50 US/$5.50 Can

RAINBOWS AND RAPTURE *by Rebecca Paisley*
76565-9/$4.50 US/$5.50 Can

AWAKEN MY FIRE *by Jennifer Horsman*
76701-5/$4.50 US/$5.50 Can

ONLY BY YOUR TOUCH *by Stella Cameron*
76606-X/$4.50 US/$5.50 Can

FIRE AT MIDNIGHT *by Barbara Dawson Smith*
76275-7/$4.50 US/$5.50 Can

ONLY WITH YOUR LOVE *by Lisa Kleypas*
76151-3/$4.50 US/$5.50 Can

MY WILD ROSE *by Deborah Camp*
76738-4/$4.50 US/$5.50 Can